Protecting Melody

Protecting Melody

SEAL of Protection
Book 7

By Susan Stoker

Table of Contents

Prologue

Six Months Ago

Tex: Hey, I haven't seen you in here before. Your username struck me as interesting, so I thought I'd shoot you a private note

Tex: Swear I'm harmless

CC_CopyCat: Hey Tex. I mostly lurk

Tex: Don't blame you, it's better to be safe than sorry

Tex: You wanna talk?

CC_CopyCat: About what?

Tex: About whatever

CC_CopyCat: That's kinda vague

Tex: Well, we could talk about the weather, but that would be cliché.

CC_CopyCat: LOL

Tex: Made ya laugh!

CC_CopyCat: Yeah, you did. Thanks

Tex: Thanks?

CC_CopyCat: Yeah. Thanks

Tex: So… how's the weather where you are?

CC_CopyCat: Crappy, you?

Tex: Sunny and beautiful

CC_CopyCat: You're one of those aren't you?

Tex: ??

CC_CopyCat: One of those annoying people who see the good side in everything

Tex: Actually, no. Not even close

Tex: You still there?

CC_CopyCat: Look, I'm not sure this is gonna work out

Tex: You just met me, I couldn't have pissed you off already

CC_CopyCat: I'm not here to find a best friend, I already have one of those

Tex: Then why ARE you here?

CC_CopyCat: Just passing the time

Tex: Then why can't you pass it with me?

CC_CopyCat: Because you're probably either a 14 year old boy who wants to find someone to sext with or you're a 50 year old pedophile looking for sex from a 16 year old teenager who doesn't know any better than to talk to people who spend their time in a chat room on the Internet.

Tex: Same goes for you. You could be anyone. You're probably an undercover cop looking to catch bad guys who use chat rooms to lure people to their death

CC_CopyCat: *ARE you a bad guy Tex? Are you even a guy?*

Tex: *Are you a woman CC?*

CC_CopyCat: *I shouldn't say one way or the other*

Tex: *No offense, but I don't want to chat with a dude. I'm not looking for a relationship, I'm not looking for sex. I have male friends I can talk to*

CC_CopyCat: *What ARE you looking for then?*

Tex: *Just someone to chat with. My life is stressful. I'd love to talk with someone who doesn't want anything from me. Who just likes to chat with me because she thinks I'm interesting*

CC_CopyCat: *You never answered my question. Are you a bad guy?*

Tex: *I'm a 35 year old retired military man who lives on the east coast. I'm good with computers and spend most of my time with them. I'm not hideous looking, but I've found that I'm also not the guy women want to take home to meet their family. Swear CC, I'm harmless.*

CC_CopyCat: *You know that's what serial killers say*

Tex: *LOL. You're right. But you can trust me*

CC_CopyCat: *Yup, they say that too*

CC_CopyCat: *You still there?*

Tex: *You gonna dis me more or are you going to tell me about you?*

CC_CopyCat: *Sorry. I was kidding. Yes. I'm a woman*

Tex: *Thank you. What else?*

CC_CopyCat: *I don't really know you, that's all you get*

Tex: *I'll take it... for now. You gonna tell me about your handle?*

CC_CopyCat: *I gotta go*

Tex: *Okay, I'll be here if you wanna talk again*

CC_CopyCat: *How will you know when I'll want to talk again?*

Tex: *I don't, but I told you I work on computers, I'm always here*

CC_CopyCat: *Okay, maybe*

Tex: *I've enjoyed talking to you CC*

CC_CopyCat: *We haven't even talked about anything interesting*

Tex: *Yeah, but you aren't afraid to tell me what you're really thinking. I like that*

CC_CopyCat: *Most men don't*

Tex: *I'm not most men*

CC_CopyCat: *Whatever. OK, I'm logging off*

Tex: *Bye CC. Later*

Tex sat back and smiled at his computer. He didn't usually engage people he met online, but he'd been visiting this particular chat room for a while now and noticed "*CC_CopyCat*" lurking. He'd taken a chance and sent the private message, hoping he was messaging a woman. Tex had been honest with her, he wasn't looking to start up an online friendship with a man.

Call him sexist, but Tex was more comfortable talking with a woman than a man. Maybe it was because he was around men all the time. It was just... different, speaking with a woman.

Ever since he'd lost part of his leg to an IED while on a SEAL mission, Tex was more comfortable talking to people behind his computer or phone. Before he was injured, he'd never had a problem attracting the ladies. He was in his mid-thirties now and still worked out every day. Physical fitness was too ingrained in him to give it up after he was injured.

While Tex knew firsthand, on the surface, women still found him attractive and they'd gladly go home with him, after getting weird looks and two less than satisfying sexual encounters, he found it more comfortable for everyone to not bother. He now took care of his needs himself. Tex knew his friends all thought he was still sexually active, but the awkward explanations about his injury and the pity fucks got old fast.

He tried not to care what people thought of his leg, but when he connected with people via his computer, he could be anonymous... whole. Talking to CC was refreshing. Tex liked it.

He hadn't lied to the woman on the other end of the computer. She intrigued him. She wasn't fawning all over him, as some women Tex had messaged in the past had. She was cautious, but he could sense her humor under her stilted words. Tex hoped she'd log back in and they could talk again, but if she didn't, he wouldn't lose any sleep. There would be more women, and he'd keep busy living vicariously through his friends' lives.

Four months ago

> **CC_CopyCat:** Hey Tex. How are you?
>
> **Tex:** Hey CC. I'm sorry, but I can't talk right now
>
> **CC_CopyCat:** Oh sorry
>
> **Tex:** It's not you. I'd rather talk to you than anyone else, but my friend's woman is in trouble and I'm trying to figure her situation out
>
> **CC_CopyCat:** That sucks.
>
> **Tex:** Yeah, her man is overseas and can't get to her. So I'm trying to get him home and keep her safe
>
> **CC_CopyCat:** OK, go do your thing. If you want to talk later, I'm here
>
> **Tex:** Thanks CC. I needed that. Later

Tex hated to put CC off. They'd been talking pretty regularly for the last two months and Tex really enjoyed their conversations, but Fiona was counting on him. She was obviously having a mental breakdown after whatever had happened in the shopping mall. He was calling her every four hours. It was heartbreaking to listen to her try to figure out what was going on—trying to decide what was real and what was imagined in her head. She was so scared. Tex turned back to the computers and typed frantically to try to get Cookie home and to his woman.

The next day, after the entire situation with Fiona was finally over, Tex tried to see if CC was around.

Tex: *You around?*

Tex: *Guess not. If you come back, I'm here*

Tex ran a hand over his face. Jesus. Fiona had just about broken his heart. He hadn't ever met her, had only met Caroline, Wolf's woman, but Fiona was just as tough, yet vulnerable at the same time, as Caroline was. She'd done exactly what he'd asked of her and every time Tex had called, she'd answered. Tex had no idea what he would've done if Fiona hadn't picked up the phone. She was in California and he was in Virginia.

Tex knew his friends had a lot of faith in his abilities, but if something had really gone wrong, there would've been nothing he could've done. Tex cursed his leg, again. Not a day went by that he didn't wish he'd have done something different on the mission that took his leg. Not a day went by that he didn't wish he was whole and the man he used to be.

He was good at the computer, but he wished with all his heart he could be on the front lines, with his friends, saving lives and serving his country. Tex looked down at the box blinking at him in the corner of his computer screen. CC.

CC_CopyCat: Hey Tex, I'm here. You there?

Tex: Yeah CC, I'm here

CC_CopyCat: Everything go OK with your friend?

Tex: Yeah

CC_CopyCat: I know we've only been talking to each other for a little while, but you're not your usual self...

Tex: CC, you have no idea

CC_CopyCat: You wanna talk about it?

Tex: You sure you want this? We can keep this light and fluffy and superficial. We can say hi every now and then and go on with our lives as we have been. But I'll tell you. I've had a tough few days and could use more than that. But if we get deeper, I can't go back to light and fluffy. You choose.

CC_CopyCat: I don't like that you've had a shit day, and I'd love to talk to you about it, but I can't give it back to you. I want to, I just can't.

Tex: It's OK. We can keep it light

CC_CopyCat: NO! Dammit Tex. You need to talk about stuff. You can't keep it in. I didn't mean that I didn't want you to talk to me

Tex: I don't need a therapist, I need a friend. I get that you're cautious and it's smart. I get it, but CC, I've enjoyed our chats over the last 2 months, but I'd like to be more real with you. We'll never meet, so I *feel safe talking to you about stuff. You can't share my secrets 'cos you don't know who I am. I can't share yours because of the same thing. Please, tell me something, <u>anything</u>, personal about yourself.*

Tex sat back and held his breath. He didn't know what it was about CC, but he really wanted to talk to her, *really* talk to her. He hadn't lied. He *had* enjoyed talking to her. They'd talked about their favorite foods (she liked Mexican, he liked Italian), favorite colors (hers was pink, his was blue), and many, many other superficial things. She'd even asked what his favorite Disney character was at one point. He'd thought it an odd question, but had answered her anyway.

But now Tex was at the point where he needed their relationship to be deeper than it was. He didn't really know why, but he wanted to get to know her better. He liked her. She was funny and interesting and even though they hadn't really talked about anything personal, he thought she'd be the kind of person he'd like to get to know better. He wasn't satisfied with the superficial stuff anymore.

Tex waited another few moments and when CC didn't respond back, he leaned forward and typed out a terse note, ready to log off and talk to her some other time.

Tex: OK then, I gotta go

CC_CopyCat: My name is Mel. It's short for Melody

9

Tex: *Thank you, Mel. You have no idea how much I needed that. Thank you*

CC_CopyCat: *Tell me about your shit day*

Tex: *A while ago, my buddy's woman was kidnapped by Mexican slave traders. She was rescued and doing great. But recently she had a flashback and ran.*

CC_CopyCat: *Jesus, Tex. But she's OK?*

Tex: *Yeah Mel, she's OK. But for three days all she had was me. I called her every 4 hours to make sure she was staying put in the hotel. I listened to her go back and forth between reality and the shit that was messing with her head.*

CC_CopyCat: *I'm proud of you Tex*

Tex: *Don't be. I've done some horrible things in my life*

CC_CopyCat: *Hasn't everyone? Seriously, get off your high horse Tex. You aren't the only person that wishes they'd done things differently. You aren't the only one who has a crap background, or crap childhood, or crap marriage. You just keep moving forward. You learn from the past and keep going. Sounds to me like your friends are lucky to have you on their side.*

CC_CopyCat: *Tex? Shit. Too real? Not fluffy enough?*

Tex: *NO. Not too real. I'm just thinking.*

CC_CopyCat: *OK. Let me know when you're done*

Tex: *Smart ass. You're right. But I think the things I did are worse than the run-of-the-mill crap background.*

CC_CopyCat: *So what. Are you going to go off and continue to do those horrible things? Sounds to me like you're trying to change that. That you're doing good. I'm sure your friend would agree with me*

Tex: *Maybe*

CC_CopyCat: *No maybe about it*

Tex: *OK, you win*

CC_CopyCat: *Of course I do*

Tex: *Mel?*

CC_CopyCat: *Yeah?*

Tex: *I'm glad you didn't choose fluffy*

CC_CopyCat: *Me too*

Two Months Ago

Tex: *Last time we talked you said you were scared all the time. I don't like that.*

CC_CopyCat: *I don't like it either*

Tex: *What are you scared of?*

CC_CopyCat: *People watching me. Getting shot. Getting kidnapped. Being sick. Being alone. You name it Tex, I'm scared of it.*

Tex: *Do you have depression Mel?*

CC_CopyCat: *No, why?*

Tex: *Most people who are scared of all those things are mentally ill*

CC_CopyCat: *So you're saying you think I'm crazy?*

Tex: You know I'm not. But I do want to know if there's something really going on with you.

CC_CopyCat: I'm not crazy or depressed

Tex: Then what?

CC_CopyCat: Never mind

Tex: No, not never mind. TALK to me. Why are you scared of those things?

CC_CopyCat: I just am

Tex: Don't bullshit me

CC_CopyCat: You ever get the feeling that you're being watched?

Tex: No

CC_CopyCat: Well, I do. And it scares me. And thinking about that makes me think about the other stuff too. It's a never-ending circle

Tex: Never take the same route when you go about your daily business. Always walk with your keys in your hand. Walk with your head up and look people in the eyes. If you get in an elevator, don't turn your back to people. Never stay in an elevator if it's only you and a man you don't know. Tell someone when you expect to be home.

CC_CopyCat: You know a lot about this

Tex: Mel, I told you I was a Navy SEAL. We spend way too much time learning this kind of shit. If you get cornered or someone attacks you, go for their eyes, or their throat, or their balls. Don't get in a car with someone if they try to take you away, you're better *off in a public place.*

CC_CopyCat: *Tex, I got it. I'm probably just imagining it anyway*

Tex: *I bet you aren't. Anytime I got in a situation where I felt weird, in 100% of the cases, it turned out I was right.*

CC_CopyCat: *OK, I'll be careful*

Tex: *If you need me, you shoot me a note, I'm here*

CC_CopyCat: *But we don't really even know each other*

Tex: *Don't care. Just agree*

CC_CopyCat: *You're awfully bossy*

Tex: *Agree*

CC_CopyCat: *OK*

Tex: *Good*

One Month Ago

CC_CopyCat: *Tell me about your friends. You talk about them all the time, and it's obvious they have some seriously awesome wives and girlfriends.*

Tex: *Yeah, they're all great. You know I was a SEAL. I worked with some of them when I was in the Navy, but after I retired they found themselves in need of my computer abilities. I can usually get them what they need faster than going through proper channels and with the issues their women have had, thank God that I can.*

CC_CopyCat: *What are their names again?*

Tex: *Wolf, Abe, Cookie, Mozart, Benny, and Dude*

CC_CopyCat: *I'm sure there's some good stories behind those names*

Tex: *Of course*

CC_CopyCat: *Who do you rely on?*

Tex: *What do you mean?*

CC_CopyCat: *When you need someone, or something, who do you rely on?*

CC_CopyCat: *Tex? Shit, sorry. Did I overstep?*

Tex: *No*

CC_CopyCat: *Forget I asked. I'm sorry*

Tex: *As weird as this might sound. You.*

CC_CopyCat: *What?*

Tex: *You, Mel. When I've had a crap day, I get on here and talk to you. You don't judge me, you don't ask me for anything, you just talk to me.*

CC_CopyCat: *I won't be around forever Tex. You need to get out more. Find someone there you can talk to.*

Tex: *People don't "see" me as you do Mel*

CC_CopyCat: *Maybe you don't give them a chance*

Tex: *No. I live in a military town. Most can tell by my limp that I'm not whole. They pity me. I can't stand pity. I was a fucking SEAL. And if I'm wearing shorts? Forget about it.*

CC_CopyCat: *Not whole? Tex. Over the last months*

of me talking to you, I can tell you're one of the most alpha men I've ever met. You're bossy and you tell me what to do all the time. But at the same time you're compassionate, you worry about your friends, and you drop everything to help them, even when they don't ask. Believe me when I say that those people who see the surface that is you aren't seeing even one tenth of who YOU are. Fuck them. See yourself as I do.

Tex: *Shit Mel*

CC_CopyCat: *No, I'm not done*

CC_CopyCat: *I think your friends take advantage of you. They're always calling you to help them. To help their women, but you haven't talked about them coming out there to see you. To thank you in person.*

Tex: *Mel, listen*

CC_CopyCat: *No*

CC_CopyCat: *You listen*

CC_CopyCat: *Tex, If you were my friend I'd never take advantage of you. Ever.*

Tex: *You <u>are</u> my friend*

CC_CopyCat: *Damn straight*

Tex: *Thanks for making me feel better*

CC_CopyCat: *Anytime*

Tex: *What about you?*

CC_CopyCat: *What about me what?*

Tex: *What about your friends?*

CC_CopyCat: *I've got friends*

Tex: *Who? You never talk about them.*

CC_CopyCat: *Amy. Amy is my friend*

Tex: *Just Amy?*

CC_CopyCat: *Yeah. I trust her with my life. I miss her though. I've been away and I haven't been able to talk to her as much as I'd like*

Tex: *Why?*

CC_CopyCat: *It's complicated*

Tex: *You see me going anywhere?*

CC_CopyCat: *Amy's back home. She has a husband and two kids and works for a contractor. She tells me all the time that her company builds stuff that kills people, but her job is to finance it. I have no idea what that means, but I laugh at her anyway.*

Tex: *She sounds funny*

CC_CopyCat: *She is! Sometimes we have complete conversations using hashtags*

Tex: *#likethis?*

CC_CopyCat: *#yeah*

Tex: *So why don't you talk to her much?*

CC_CopyCat: *Well, she's home, and has a life to live. And I'm not there, so it's just hard.*

Tex: *I won't push, but that sounds like a cop out*

Tex: *I know you're not telling me the entire story, and I don't like it. But as I said, I won't push. But I AM going to send you my cell phone number. You don't ever have to use it, but I want you to have it in case you want to ever talk. I think we're good enough* *friends now that we can move our online relationship to the next level. I'd love to hear your voice sometime. I feel like your friend too. So, what are you doing today?*

CC_CopyCat: *Well, you know I work from wherever I am, so I've got two jobs today and otherwise I'm just hanging out. You?*

Tex: *I'm going to check in with my friends and make sure all is calm there, then I think I'm going to do something crazy today.*

CC_CopyCat: *What's that?*

Tex: *There's a new thriller out I've been meaning to read*

CC_CopyCat: *LOL. Crazy day for you*

Tex: *You know it*

CC_CopyCat: *Seriously Tex, you need to get out and interact with people more*

Tex: *Pot meet kettle*

CC_CopyCat: *Yeah, but you're you. I haven't seen a picture of you, but I bet you're beautiful. You're probably tall and built. Your hair is probably a bit too long and there's not one woman who passes you who doesn't take a second look.*

Tex: *Men aren't beautiful*

CC_CopyCat: *The hell they aren't*

Tex: *Well, I'm not. I don't think my hair is too long, but the only reason women take a second glance at me is to pity me because of my injuries*

CC_CopyCat: *You're wrong. I'm 100% sure you're wrong. Next time you're out, look. REALLY look. I bet you'd be surprised.*

CC_CopyCat: *Hey, I hate to do this, but I gotta go. I have a thing in twenty minutes and I have to get ready.*

Tex: *OK Melody. As usual I've enjoyed talking to you*

CC_CopyCat: *Yeah, me too. You have no idea how much. I was serious about what I said Tex. You need to get out more. Find that woman who's meant to be yours. You deserve it just as much as your friends and I'm sure they'd say the same thing.*

Tex: *I'll try. Talk later?*

CC_CopyCat: *Yeah*

Tex: *OK, bye. Have a good day*

CC_CopyCat: *You too. Bye*

Chapter One

T EX PACED HIS apartment. He wasn't happy. He couldn't get hold of Melody. It wasn't unusual for them to go a couple days without talking, but it had been a week. Ever since he'd first messaged her all those months ago, they hadn't gone that long without touching base. Tex looked down at his computer screen. The words there mocked him.

> **Tex:** *Mel? Are you there? Haven't heard from you in awhile*
>
> **Tex:** *I'm worried about you. Please. Talk to me. I miss your sarcasm*
>
> **Tex:** *If you don't answer me, I'm going to have to make <u>sure</u> you're all right. I know you never wanted to talk on the phone, or exchange photos, but I have to know you're okay. I've already given you my cell number, please call or text me.*

Tex had no idea when Melody had become so important to him. There were many nights he'd stayed up late talking with her online. She was funny and sarcastic, but she got him in a way his Navy SEAL friends never would. Tex had opened up to Mel about how insecure he felt around women after his operation and how he hadn't taken off his prosthetic in front of anyone other than his doctors.

Tex knew it was the security of typing rather than talking face-to-face or even on the phone that made him open up to Melody. There was some safety in the anonymity of the Internet and writing what he felt rather than talking about it. Even the Navy shrinks had tried to get him to open up and he couldn't.

But with Melody he was able to, and had. She knew everything about him. And now that he hadn't talked to her in seven long days, Tex was realizing how little he actually knew about her. He'd blown it off in the past, not really thinking too much about it. He knew Mel got very defensive every time he tried to get her to talk about herself, so he'd dropped it. Tex didn't want to scare her off, he enjoyed talking to her too much.

But now, he was kicking himself. He knew almost nothing about her, and he was worried.

Tex looked back down at his computer screen. He clicked some buttons, then just stared at the chat box he'd just been using to talk to Mel.

User unknown.

Tex sat up abruptly in his chair and frantically

clicked more buttons. He swore long, using some of the more inventive words he'd learned during his time on the teams. Melody had deleted her account. She wasn't just logged off; she'd severed the only connection they had with each other.

Something was more than wrong. While Tex didn't know the specifics of her life, he knew enough to know she wouldn't just up and disappear without a word to him… unless something was really wrong.

Tex tried to remember every piece of information she'd let slip over the last few months. He opened a new document and started typing.

Pink
Mexican food
Disney?
Friend named Amy – works in contracting – govt?
Works from home – jobs that start at specific
times
Time difference? Job starting at 10pm my time
CC_CopyCat – has to mean something, but what?
Being watched? Scared

Tex sat back and stared at the list he'd made. It wasn't a lot of information. Hell, it was shit. But he didn't like what it was adding up to. His Mel was on the run. He had no idea from what or who, but it was suddenly as clear as if she'd whispered the words across the globe and they'd landed in his ear.

Mel was cautious, not wanting to tell him anything about her. She didn't talk to her best friend, even though it was obvious she was longing to. She was scared and felt like she was being watched. Whatever she did to earn money, she was able to do it on the road, she didn't work a traditional job.

Melody had his phone number, but Tex didn't think she'd use it. She was too concerned about taking advantage of people and was too scared of something. And if she wouldn't call him, and Tex figured if she hadn't called her friend Amy so far, she wouldn't break that pattern now. Mel probably wasn't in contact with her friend because she was afraid whatever situation she was in would blow back on her.

Tex rolled up his sleeves. Fuck that. He'd never felt like this about anyone in his entire life. He felt like if he didn't find Melody, a huge piece of his life would be missing. Over the last six months she'd come to mean a lot to him. Tex didn't know how it happened, but it had. He had no idea what she looked like, but knew it didn't matter. She could weigh five hundred pounds or be sixty years old, but she was his friend and Tex needed to find and help her.

It was as if his entire life he'd been leading up to this moment. He'd found his friends' women, he could find Melody. For one of the first times in his life, Tex was going to concentrate on himself. He wasn't thinking about his friends, he wasn't thinking about his leg or the constant pain he felt. He had to find and help Melody.

TEX RUBBED HIS hand over his face. What time was it? What *day* was it? He had no idea, but he thought he'd *finally* tracked down Melody's friend, Amy. He wasn't sure, but it was worth a shot. He'd combed through contracting agencies throughout the country trying to narrow them down based on what Melody had told him Amy did. Tex hadn't been surprised at how many Amys worked for the government. He'd called about two hundred so far and while some people would call him crazy for thinking he could find a needle in a haystack, he felt good about *this* Amy.

Tex picked up the phone and dialed the number he had for Amy Smith. It was almost cliché with her having the surname of "Smith." It had made it that much harder to pin her down.

"Hello?"

"Is this Amy Smith who works for Key Contracting?"

"Who the hell is this?"

"I'm a friend of Melody's and… hello?" Tex looked down at the phone in his hand when suddenly all he heard was the dial tone. He couldn't help but be impressed and he felt in his gut this *was* Melody's friend. All of the other Amys he'd reached had spoken with him politely and had said they didn't know anyone with the name of Melody. But *this* Amy had hung up at the mere mention of Mel's name.

If Melody was in as much trouble as Tex thought she was, her friend had done the right thing, but that didn't mean it didn't still piss him off. He immediately dialed the number again and wasn't surprised when Amy didn't pick up the phone. He left a quick message.

"My name is Tex. I'm a retired Navy SEAL. I've been talking to Mel online for the last six months and she's told me about you. I'm afraid she's in trouble. I haven't talked to her in ten days and I'm worried. Please call me back. Hashtag, your friend needs help."

Tex had no idea if what he'd said was enough, but he gambled that Amy hearing he was a SEAL might change her mind toward him. But if that didn't do it, maybe his last hashtag comment would.

His phone rang six minutes after he left the message, he'd been counting. Tex picked it up, recognizing the number.

"What the hell is going on?" Amy didn't waste any time with niceties.

"As I said, I've been talking to Mel online for a while now. She never told me anything about her personal life, but I'm worried about her. We usually talk at least once a week, but I haven't heard from her in a week and a half."

"Look, no offense, but I don't know you. How do I know you aren't the one stalking her?"

"So she's being stalked?"

"Fuck."

Tex heard the disgust in Amy's voice. She hadn't meant to confirm anything. "Look…" Tex paused and thought about what he could say to try to reassure Melody's friend. "I know she's scared. She admitted as much to me. She talked about you when I asked about her friends. She said she misses you. Amy, I need your help. I need you to tell me everything you can about where you think she is. She's obviously in trouble and she needs help. I can help her."

"Give me your name. I'll check you out. If I think you're legit, I'll call you back."

Tex didn't hesitate. "John Keegan. I was medically retired a few years ago from the Navy. Do you need a reference?"

"No. I'll find you if you're telling me the truth. I have my own connections."

Tex put the phone down. Amy had hung up without saying goodbye once again. He didn't care. All that mattered was Melody. Now that he knew he had the right Amy, Tex bent over his computer again. He could find out a lot of information now that he verified where Melody was from.

Thirty minutes later, Tex's phone rang. Impatiently he picked it up and answered the call, figuring it would be Amy. She obviously *did* have some good contacts if she was already calling him back and had checked him out this quickly.

Amy didn't bother saying hello. "My friend, Melody, was the nicest person you could ever meet. She was the type of person who would come over and watch my kids for free, and, in fact, beg me to be able to do it. She babysat my kids all the time and they loved her. She worked hard at what she did and she was good at it. She didn't bad mouth others and was way nicer than she should've been to people."

"Why are you talking about her in the past tense?" It shouldn't have struck Tex as so wrong to hear Amy talking about Melody as if she was no longer alive, but it did.

Amy's voice softened for the first time. "I didn't even realize I was doing it."

"How long has she been gone?" Tex tried to ease up on his take-charge attitude. Amy was obviously hurting too.

"About seven or so months."

"Have you talked to her much since she's been gone?"

"Not really, and it sucks. I miss her. My kids miss her. Her parents miss her. Hell, her *dog* misses her."

"Her dog?" Tex didn't remember Melody ever talking about owning a dog in any of their past conversations.

"Yeah. She asked if I would dogsit one day because she had to run some errands in Pittsburgh. So I took Baby for the day and Melody never came back."

"Her dog's name is Baby?" Tex could hear that Amy was getting emotional and he wanted to have her concentrate on something else for a moment before she continued telling him about Melody.

"Yeah. Baby is a fifty pound coonhound. Melody adores that dog. Every time I've spoken with her since she left, which isn't very often, she's asked about her dog. Baby misses her too. It's uncanny. She lays on the floor each night and keeps her eyes on the door. She knows. Even after all these months, Baby knows her mom is missing and is still waiting for her to walk back through the door."

"What happened? Why did Melody go? What's she told you?" Tex knew he sounded gruff, but he couldn't help it. He needed all the information he could get from Amy to help him find Melody. And the thought of Mel's dog pining for her made his stomach clench and hurt him more than if Amy had described how much she herself missed her friend.

"I don't know all the details because Melody won't tell me, but from what I can gather, she'd been receiving weird notes for a while. Not necessarily threatening, but not friendly either. Then they changed. The messages got mean. Melody didn't tell me exactly what they said, but I think they started threatening her parents and even Baby. She told me once that if it was just her, she never would've left. And I believe that with all my heart."

"Because if it was just her, she wouldn't care, but threaten someone or something she loves, and all bets are off." Tex could see Melody being that way. Again, he'd only been acquainted with her for a short while, but with the way she supported him and stood up for him when she didn't really even know him, Tex knew she'd be horrified by the thought of someone getting hurt because of her.

"Yeah." Amy's voice was low. "You *do* know her."

"Yeah. I know her."

"I'm worried, Tex. I haven't talked to her in about three months, and the last time I spoke with her she didn't sound good."

"In what way?"

"Usually she tries to be happy and cheerful when she talks to me, but last time she didn't try to hide her feelings. She was scared and depressed. She told me over and over how much she loved me and the kids and told me to give Baby extra pets for her." Amy took a deep breath. "When she said good-bye, it sounded different than any other time."

"It sounded final."

"Exactly. I tried to keep her on the phone, but she said she had to go and she hung up."

"I'm going to find her, Amy."

"She's going to be scared when you do. Someone's after her. If you're telling the truth and she doesn't know what you look like, she's gonna run."

"She won't run when she sees me."

"You sound sure of yourself."

"I am." Tex didn't elaborate.

"Please bring her home."

"I will. Can I ask a favor?" Tex knew what he was going to ask was highly unusual and Amy would most likely need some convincing, but after speaking with her he knew it was the right move and something he had to do.

After Amy agreed to his favor, with a few conditions, Tex hung up. Amy had given him a lot of great information, including Melody's last name, Grace, and Tex knew it was only a matter of time before he found her. And when he did, he'd make sure she was safe and could go home again.

Chapter Two

T EX SMILED OVER at the coonhound sitting next to
him in his truck. Baby was sitting on her haunches,
almost like a human would, with her nose in the air
sniffing the breeze coming in through the open window.
Tex wasn't a dog expert, but for some reason he *needed*
to pick up Baby and bring her with him on his quest to
find Melody.

He had a connection with Melody, and having her
beloved dog next to him made Tex feel closer to her.
Besides, Baby was the cutest thing he'd ever seen, it
wasn't as if it was a hardship to have her along for the
ride. She had legs that seemed too long for her frame.
Her paws were big, but she was lean. She was tan and
white, with most of her belly being white and the
majority of her back and head being tan. Baby's ears
hung low, not quite as long as a basset hound or blood-
hound's might, but they made her face look perpetually
sad. But it was her eyes that had solidified Tex's decision
to take her with him. They were a unique shade of

brown, if Tex had to describe it, he'd say they were the color of amber. Every time she looked at him it was as if she saw right through him to all his fears and insecurities and could somehow make them all disappear.

Luckily, Baby had taken to him right away. She'd walked up to him as if she'd known him her entire life and had sat down right on his foot. Tex ruffled her ears and Baby looked up at him with the most trusting look Tex had ever seen. It was as if the dog knew Tex was there to take her to Melody.

On the phone, Amy had agreed to let him take Melody's dog, but it had taken some convincing once he'd arrived at her home. Tex had told Amy he'd drive up to Bethel Park, Pennsylvania and collect Baby. After he'd arrived, Tex spent an uncomfortable two hours with Amy and her family. They'd asked a million questions, and given him a thousand directions on what Baby liked and how to care for her.

When all was said and done, Amy had given Tex a hug and simply whispered in his ear before he left, "I'm only letting you take Baby because I know you're gonna find Melody. Bring my friend home, Tex. Please."

So here he was. Tex had packed two laptops, a large duffle bag and headed north to Pennsylvania. Now he had a large bag of premium dog food, an assortment of dog toys and snacks, and a dog to add to his belongings.

Tex was headed to California. It was a long drive

from one side of the country to the other, but he was used to small amounts of sleep. He didn't plan on making very many stops, counting on arriving in California in about three days. He wanted to be there immediately, knowing every day that passed with no communication with Melody meant one more day she could be in trouble. Making the stop in Pennsylvania meant Tex lost a day, but he didn't want to leave Baby behind.

His sixth sense was screaming at him to take the dog with him, and he never ignored that feeling. It had saved him and his SEAL teammates more than once. Tex had no idea why it was important, other than the fact he knew Melody loved her dog.

His plan was to take Interstate 70 across the United States until St. Louis, then cut down to Interstate 40 to Barstow, California, then finally head south on Interstate 15 into the Los Angeles area.

Tex was more certain he was on the right track in finding where Melody was hiding after his trip to Pennsylvania. Putting together all the things he'd gleaned from his conversations with Melody herself and from talking with Amy, he believed she was hiding on the west coast.

He'd done a lot of research online before heading to Pennsylvania and Amy's house. He'd tracked Mel's movements when she left home. She went south first and then west to California. Most of the things he'd done to get that far weren't legal, but Tex was used to getting what he wanted, and covering his tracks while he was doing it.

Los Angeles was a huge city, and it was a long shot that Tex would find her quickly, but he was going to start with the Anaheim area. Melody had asked about his favorite Disney character, it had been an odd thing to ask out of the blue. Tex had asked Amy if Melody had a "thing" for Disney and she'd said no. So Tex could only conclude that Melody asking, had to have something to do with what she was seeing on a daily basis.

Amy had also told Tex that Melody was a Closed Caption reporter. It fit. She could work on the road from anywhere that had an Internet connection. There weren't that many CC companies in the country and Tex knew he could further track her that way. While it'd be more difficult because Melody was obviously using public Wi-Fi to connect, Tex could still narrow down the area where she was by backtracking the connection.

Tex was also happy to be headed to the Los Angeles area because he'd get a chance to catch up with his friends and to meet all their women. He felt as if he already knew them, and he couldn't wait to meet them face-to-face. While he wanted to rush and find Melody, he also knew he'd have to take at least one night's break to take care of his leg. Tex figured he'd drop down to Riverton and visit with Wolf and the rest of the team before heading back up to LA to find Melody.

He'd called the night before and told Wolf he was on his way west. Tex smiled remembering the shriek of joy that had come out of Caroline when Wolf had told her he was on his way to California.

Tex remembered Melody commenting on how she thought his friends were taking advantage of him. He knew that wasn't the case, but it felt good to have Melody looking out for him. Wolf had told him everyone had been planning on flying out to Virginia in a few months to visit. When Tex had asked who "everyone" was, he'd been shocked to hear it was *all* of them. Wolf, Caroline, Abe, Alabama, Cookie, Fiona, Mozart, Summer, Dude, Cheyenne, Benny, and Jessyka were all going to take a week off and come out to Virginia to see him. Tex almost couldn't believe it. It was ridiculous for all of them to fly to him, when he could more easily go out to California to see all of them.

Wolf had just laughed and said, "Try telling our women that."

Tex loved his friends' women. They were tough as hell, but more importantly, they made his friends happy. Tex felt proud he had a hand in keeping them safe, and he'd continue to do it as long as they'd let him.

He knew he came off as somewhat of a hard-ass on the phone when he'd had the pleasure of speaking with his friends' women, but he wasn't sure what to expect when he met them in person. While he was still a SEAL and knew how to kill someone with his bare hands, losing part of his leg had changed him fundamentally. Over the phone or on the computer, he could be the man he used to be, but in person, he couldn't help but wonder if people thought he was weak. And that uncertainty had seeped into his psyche.

Even with Tex's excitement in being able to see his friends again, he had mixed feelings about this trip west. There was no doubt he'd have a great time with the group, but his main goal was to find Melody and figure out what was going on with her.

Baby woofed in the seat next to Tex.

"Need to stretch your legs, Baby?"

Baby just looked at him, head cocked.

"Yeah, okay, let me find a place to stop. I could use a break too."

Tex pulled over at the next rest area along the Interstate and clipped a leash onto Baby's collar. There was no way he wanted to risk losing Melody's dog. Tex knew hounds were prone to follow their nose instead of commands and because they were in the middle of Indiana surrounded by trees, Tex didn't want Baby to get the scent of a rabbit and take off.

Baby jumped out of the truck after Tex and happily trotted after him as they walked around the grassy area. Baby did her business and didn't protest when Tex steered her back to the truck. She jumped into the cab as if she'd done it a million times before. Tex unclipped the leash and left her in the truck with the windows cracked so he could go inside.

When he came back outside five minutes later, Baby was sitting in the passenger's side of the truck as if she was waiting for him.

"Ready to go find Melody?" Tex felt silly talking to a dog, but as if she could understand him, Baby woofed once and put her paw on his arm. Tex scratched behind Baby's ear and started the truck. They had a long way to go.

TEX PULLED INTO Wolf's driveway and shut off the engine. He was tired. His leg hurt, well it always hurt, but sitting in the truck for three days straight hadn't done it any good. As much as it'd pained him, Tex had bypassed Los Angeles to head down to San Diego to see his friends and their women. It wasn't much of a detour, and even though Tex wanted to see Wolf and the others, it was tough to put off his search for Melody for even one day, even though that had been his plan all along.

Tex ran his hand over Baby's head, which was resting on his thigh. Tex never had a dog growing up, but over the last three days he'd fallen in love with Baby. She was an easy dog to love. Mild-mannered, non-demanding, and she minded surprisingly well for a hound.

"We made it, Baby. Ready to meet my friends?" As had become his habit, Tex told Baby everything they were going to do before they did it. Tex opened his door and Baby was immediately ready to go. She sat in the driver's seat until Tex clipped the leash onto her collar and then happily jumped down next to him.

Tex limped up to the front door, realizing suddenly that he probably should've stayed in a hotel for one more night rather than bothering his friends at this hour, but it was too late now. The door flung open and Caroline was running toward him.

Tex stopped and braced himself, ready to catch the woman hurdling herself at him, but Caroline didn't bowl him over. Baby shifted until she was standing in front of him and growled, a low menacing sound that Tex had never heard out of the dog in the time he'd been around her. Caroline stopped suddenly and Tex looked down in bewilderment. Baby had never shown one ounce of aggression toward anyone in the last three days. She'd sat next to him for thousands of miles and hadn't growled or barked the entire trip. They'd seen countless of strangers along the way and Baby had never cared. There was even one rest stop that was crowded with rough and mean looking bikers, and Baby hadn't even spared them a second glance. But she certainly cared now.

"Holy cow!" Caroline said breathlessly, then Wolf was there. He curled one arm around Caroline's waist and pulled her behind him, and away from the growling dog.

"Baby! No!" Tex commanded gruffly.

The coonhound didn't completely back off, but she did sit down on top of Tex's foot. He could tell she wasn't relaxed. Every muscle in her body was ready to attack, to protect.

"Nice dog you got there, Tex," Wolf said sarcastically.

"Sorry about this. She's been perfectly fine the entire trip."

"I ran up at you, Tex. She's protecting you. You've trained her well," Caroline said humor lacing her voice.

"She's not my dog and I didn't train her. I just met her three days ago." Tex couldn't understand why Baby was acting like she was, but he couldn't help but be flattered. Apparently Baby had adopted him as a de facto master. Her loyalty to him felt good.

"Well, it looks like the time you spent with her on the road cemented your relationship in her mind. She's certainly claimed you, and I agree with Ice. She's protecting you," Wolf noted dryly.

Tex leaned over at the waist, knowing if he crouched down he'd never be able to get up again with his bum leg. He took hold of Baby's scruff with one hand and put the other under her chin and forced her head up so she was looking at him. "It's okay, Baby. These are my friends. They'll be Melody's friends too once we find her. You can't bite them. Hell, you probably shouldn't even growl at them."

Tex ran his hand over the dog's head as he let go of her. Baby licked his hand once, and her tail started wagging again.

"Do you think I can give you a hug now or is she gonna go for my jugular?" Caroline joked.

"Come here, woman," Tex told her in response and reached out and pulled Caroline to him.

When Baby didn't growl or in any other way show aggression, Caroline relaxed in his arms.

"It's so fucking good to see you, Ice. It's been way too long. You keeping Wolf in line?"

"Hell, Tex. You know that's an impossible task," Caroline joked back. "Come on, let's go inside and get you settled. I'm sure you're tired and want to crash for a few hours. We've got the basement all ready for you."

Tex pulled back and smiled at Caroline. She was always wanting to take care of people. He snapped his fingers at Baby as he started walking. Even though he had the leash in his hand, he was trying to teach her to respond to his nonverbal commands. So far, Baby was doing a hell of a good job at it too. The dog was smart. Very smart.

As they walked, Wolf clasped Tex on the shoulder. "Good to see you, man. Drive out okay?"

"Yeah, long, but good."

The two men looked at each other and Wolf recognized Tex's sign of "later." Tex didn't want to worry Caroline about how he was really feeling or about Melody either. Tex had told Wolf a little bit about what he was doing in California, but not the entire story.

They entered the small house and Baby trotted alongside Tex as if she'd known him her entire life. He unclipped the leash as soon as the front door closed behind them. Baby continued to stick close to Tex, not exploring the house or otherwise even looking like she was curious about where they were. She had eyes only for Tex.

After sitting at the kitchen table for about thirty minutes, and some general conversation, Caroline called it a night. She kissed Tex on the forehead and lovingly ran her hand over her husband's head before she left the room. Baby lifted her head and watched Caroline leave the room, but she didn't otherwise move from her spot at Tex's feet.

The men watched as Caroline disappeared from view, and they waited another couple of minutes. Finally Wolf spoke.

"Talk to me. What's going on? I know you. You wouldn't drive across the country on a whim. What's this girl to you?"

"Wolf, I've never met her, but she's in trouble."

"Don't get me wrong. I hate to see women hurting or in trouble myself, but it sounds like you're in deep with this woman you don't even know. It's odd."

"I said I've never met her," Tex repeated, "not that I don't know her. I've been talking to this woman for the last six months. She's in trouble and I have to help her."

"Okay, tell me what the team can do."

Tex smiled. He missed being a part of the teams. He remembered the instant loyalty and how no one ever questioned another when it was obvious they knew something was off or that it felt right.

"Honestly? I don't know. I'm operating on a hunch at this point. I don't even know if Melody is even *in* Anaheim."

"You know it's only a short trip up there if you need us. I'll let the Commander know that we might need to bug out for a few days if you need us."

"Thanks, Wolf, I appreciate it."

"Speaking of the Commander, he wasn't thrilled you sicced Julie Lytle on him."

Tex grinned. "Hey, I heard she wanted to talk to Cookie. I figured it'd be good for both of them if she was able to move on from what happened in Mexico."

"You know the Commander and her are together now don't you?" Wolf asked.

Tex simply raised his eyebrows at Wolf.

"Of course you do. Jesus, Tex. I shouldn't be surprised at who you know and how you have an uncanny ability to know what people need before they know they need it, but I still always am."

"Seriously," Tex commented, "I didn't know they'd end up together, but if anyone needed some luck in their life, it was Julie. And if Hurt is happy, more power to him. And I fully intend to call in my marker from the Commander if Melody needs it."

"Of course. I know he won't hesitate to do whatever it is to help you out. You know every one of us on the team owes you. Big." Knowing if he continued along that vein, Tex wouldn't appreciate it, Wolf changed the subject. "You taking the dog with you? You can leave her here if you want to."

"Thanks, but I'll keep her with me."

Baby looked up as if she could tell the men were talking about her and whined. Tex put his hand down and placed it on Baby's head.

"Okay, go on and get some sleep then. Just to give you a head's up, Caroline's invited the entire clan over for breakfast tomorrow. I know you're anxious to get on the road, but I'd appreciate it if you stuck around for a bit. They all want to meet you face-to-face."

Tex sighed in mock aggravation. Truth of the matter was, he was looking forward to meeting all the women as well. "I guess I can spare a few hours."

Wolf laughed as he stood up. "See you in the morning then. I think Ice bought enough food for you to live in the basement for months, but if there's something you need that's not down there, help yourself up here. I'll go out and get your bag."

"Appreciate it." And Tex did. His leg hurt and he needed to get off it for a while. "There's a bag of dog food out there too. Baby'll need it in the morning."

Wolf lifted a hand as he went out the door, not stopping, but acknowledging Tex's words.

"Need to go out once more, Baby?" Tex asked the dog at his feet. When Baby didn't move, but instead lay down with a sigh, Tex took that as a negative on the trip outside. "Then let's go catch some sleep. It's gonna be insane around here in the morning. Those women are crazy." His words were mocking, but the tone was affectionate.

Tex painfully pushed up from the chair at the table and made his way to the basement door. As he started down the stairs, Baby was right by his side. Tex stumbled once, but because Baby was there, pushing all her weight into his good leg, she righted his balance and he didn't fall. "Thanks, girl."

After Wolf brought his bag down the stairs, and Tex had visited the bathroom, he removed his prosthetic and massaged his stump with the lotion he always carried. It hurt more than usual because of the time spent immobile on the trip cross country.

Baby jumped up into the bed next to him. She turned in what seemed like ten circles before she finally deemed her "nest" complete. She sighed once and put her head on Tex's leg. He leaned down and patted her on the head. "Good girl."

Hoping against hope, Tex leaned over and grabbed his laptop off the bedside table where he'd placed it before taking off his prosthetic. He flipped it open and turned it on, waiting for Wolf's Wi-Fi to connect.

Tex logged into the chat room he and Melody had been using and waited, hoping she'd logged back on. He'd been checking every night, just in case. After a few minutes he sighed, disappointed. She hadn't… at least she hadn't joined back up with the same username she'd used in the past. If she was on with a different name, Tex had no idea what it was and no one sent him a private message either. Tex turned off the laptop and put it back on the table. He lay back on the bed and stared at the ceiling.

He had no idea where Melody was or what she was

going through, but he hoped wherever it was, she was safe. She needed to stay that way until Tex could get to her. There was no doubt in his mind that he *would* get to her. He had to. There was no other option.

Chapter Three

TEX SMILED AS he drove away from Wolf's house. The last three hours had been crazy, but he wouldn't have missed it for the world. He hadn't forgotten Melody or why he was in California, but meeting the women had been better than he could have imagined.

As soon as he stepped foot in the kitchen he had to get through the women crying all over him. Fiona had grabbed onto him first and simply sobbed. Tex felt as if he had the most connection with her. He'd talked to her for three days in a row, every four hours, while Cookie and the team had done their best to get back into the country from a mission. Even though Fiona had been hallucinating, she remembered every word of every conversation they'd had.

She whispered in his ear as Tex held her, "Thank you for holding on to me when Hunter wasn't here to do it."

Tex had given her a big squeeze and whispered back,

"Anytime you need me, I'm here."

The other women had all taken their turn and hugged him tightly. Tex had a hand in their men being able to find them all and rescue them from horrible situations. Jessyka had even whispered to him before letting him pull away, "Thank you for convincing the guys they needed those tracker thingies too."

After Jess had been lured away by an ex who'd kidnapped Benny, she'd railed at the SEALs for not protecting themselves, and she'd been right. The only reason she'd been taken by her ex was because she'd been protecting Benny. While the SEALs had Tex make tracking devices for their women, they hadn't bothered with the same for themselves.

The men had just shook their heads at the women's emotional reactions to meeting Tex. Breakfast had been full of laughter and reminiscing of the good times in their lives. Baby had been slipped way too many pieces of bacon and sausage, but never left Tex's side for more than a moment.

Finally, Tex knew it was time to go. As much as he wanted to soak in the happiness that oozed from every pore of his friends' bodies, he couldn't get Melody out of his mind. She was out there... somewhere. She had no one. No friends like this to have her back. No military buddies to help her out. She was scared, she'd said it herself. And Tex hated that.

So as much as he loved being around Caroline and the other women, he had to go. Baby stood up as soon as he had and pranced to the door. It looked like she was just as ready to go as he was.

Now Tex's mind was going a mile a minute. He didn't really have a plan, except to head to Anaheim and see what he could find. He'd check the hotels and see if Melody had checked in. Of course that would assume she used her real name, Melody Grace, but that was unlikely. He had a photo of her Amy had given him that he could show hotel clerks, but again, they saw so many tourists that they'd probably not be able to recognize Melody from a photo. Tex would probably have to keep relying on his computer skills to narrow down her location, but he felt better knowing he was at least hopefully in the same city as she was.

After a couple of hours of driving through the city traffic, Tex pulled into a hotel only blocks from the large amusement park. Everywhere he looked he was reminded where he was. There were Disney characters everywhere. It verified his belief that when Melody had asked him about his favorite character, it was because it was an easy topic of conversation.

Tex checked in, making sure to get a room on the bottom floor so it'd be easier to walk Baby. He brought his bag in, as well as Baby's food and toys. He didn't bother with the dog bed, knowing Baby would just jump up on the mattress next to him to sleep. Tex put a bowl of water on the floor and smiled as Baby helped herself.

He sat at the table in the corner of the room by the window and plugged in his laptop. Tex was going to start with the closed caption companies and see what he could narrow down.

After thirty minutes of research and searching, he sat back in the chair. He was close. Very close. He felt it in his bones. It was easy enough to find the company Melody worked for. Just that day Melody had translated a graduation back in Indiana. Apparently the way it worked was whoever hired the service would hook up via Skype. Melody would watch the event, in this case, a graduation, and she would type out whatever was being said. Then whomever was at the graduation who needed the service would use an app and watch her typed words scroll across their smartphone screen as they sat in the audience.

It really was amazing, and it was something Tex had never really thought about before. No wonder Mel could type so fast when they were talking. He'd always wondered, but never thought to ask.

Since Melody had been online that day translating the graduation ceremony back in Indiana, Tex could trace the Wi-Fi signal back to one of two places in Anaheim. Goosebumps broke out over his skin. He was close. He absently rubbed his left thigh, trying to rub out the phantom pain that was always present. With this bit of news, it looked like a good time to head out for a cup of coffee. If Melody felt safe enough to use the internet once today, he hoped she would again.

MELODY SAT AGAINST the wall of her hotel room, behind the bed, with her knees drawn up in front of her. She held her cell phone clenched in one hand and had her head resting on her knees. It was time to move on, but she'd been in California for so long now that she really didn't want to go. If Melody was honest with herself, all she wanted to do was go home.

But whoever was stalking her had found her again, and was even more relentless than before. Melody thought she was being smart by switching hotel rooms every week and using a different hot-spot for her Internet connection, but whoever was stalking her was apparently smarter than she'd given him credit for. Melody had no idea how he was finding her, but she was tired of it all. She missed Amy. She missed Baby. She missed her parents. She missed Pennsylvania.

Melody stared at the letter that sat in the middle of the floor where she'd dropped it after reading it. The front desk clerk had given it to her as she came in that day, and Melody knew she really wouldn't like what was in it. Once she'd closed the door to the hotel room, Melody had reluctantly opened the note. She'd never forget the words.

No matter where you go, I'll find you. We're the same, you and I, why can't you see that?

Melody had no idea what it meant. This note was just as creepy as all the others. But there was no post-mark on it. Whoever had sent it to her, had walked into the hotel and handed it to the clerk. That meant he was here. That also meant Melody had to go. Now.

Melody put her head back down on her knees. She was out of ideas. Well, she had one more idea, but she had to gather up the courage to follow up on it. She squeezed the phone in her hand harder. She'd bought a bunch of disposable phones to use to call her family and Amy. She'd seen enough shows on television to know they were untraceable. It obviously didn't matter now though. He'd found her anyway.

Melody picked up her head once again, held the phone up and looked at it. She'd memorized the phone number Tex had given her. She never had any inten-tions of calling him, but she'd memorized it anyway.

She was so tempted. Melody thought back to their conversations. Tex was a good guy. He oozed good guy through every pore in his body. He was an honest-to-God-hero and Melody needed a hero, but she didn't want to drag him down, and she knew she would. He'd get so embroiled in her situation and he'd want to "fix" it, but Melody had no idea how he could.

But she was tired and scared. She had money, thanks to her closed caption jobs and with Amy's help, to move on, but to where? To another hotel in another city where the same pattern would play out? She was as far away from Pennsylvania as she could be, but somehow whoever was stalking her had still found out where she was.

Melody absently opened the text app on the phone and slowly, number by number, pushed in the number she'd memorized. Then, without thinking, she typed out the first thing she thought of.

Putting the phone down on the floor without hitting send, Melody put her head on her knees again. Her dyed brown hair fell in waves around her head and spilled down her legs. She mentally argued with herself. *What would it hurt to send the text? It's not like Tex knows where I am. I miss him. I miss talking to him. He's kept me sane this last year. He made me feel normal.*

But what if he's mad I deleted my account on the chat site? What if he doesn't answer back? But what if he does? I need to feel connected to someone for just a little bit. I need to feel not so alone. He's a SEAL. He can help me.

Without thinking more about it, Melody picked up the phone and hit send. The two words she'd written seemed garish on the small screen, but summed up all her riotous emotions so well. Would Tex respond? Would he care? Melody put her head back on her knees and closed her eyes, afraid to hope, afraid to move, afraid to stay.

TEX SAT AT the table in the little café across from the bookstore watching and waiting. Baby lay at his feet, her eyes seemingly also focused on the store across the street. It was as if she somehow knew Melody was nearby.

Tex was nervous, and he never got nervous. He was always known as the stoic one. The one who never broke a sweat before or during a mission. But Tex wasn't stoic now. He knew he was cutting it close. Melody deleting her account, the silence, the working so many jobs in a short period of time. She was getting ready to run and he needed to catch up with her before she did. He hoped like hell she'd be working another job today. She'd done an excellent job of keeping her exact whereabouts hidden, but Tex knew if he could find her, so could a stalker.

The thought of somebody terrorizing someone as sweet as Melody cut through Tex like a knife. There weren't a lot of truly "nice" people in this world, and from what he knew of Melody, she was one of them. Her family and friends couldn't think of one bad thing to say about her. Hell, even her dog was pining for her.

It pissed him off that someone would dare to terrorize somebody as sweet as Melody.

If he was honest with himself, Tex was a little freaked about how much he cared about this woman. A woman he'd never actually met. It was frankly a little crazy. Melody had told him she was twenty-seven, and in all honesty, that was probably younger than what he was really looking for in a woman. He was thirty-five, a very ancient thirty-five, but it wasn't like he was actually looking to start something with her... or was he?

Tex leaned forward and pulled out his wallet and took out the picture Amy had given him. It was of Amy and Melody. They had their arms around each other and were smiling at the camera. The women were wearing shorts and T-shirts and Amy had told him it was taken at a barbeque she had at her house not too long before Melody disappeared.

Tex ran his fingers over Melody's face. He hadn't really thought much about what Mel would actually look like. He'd liked her for her wit and her sarcasm. Tex enjoyed talking to her and knew no matter what she looked like, he would still enjoy talking to her. But as it turned out, Melody was cute. Her hair was blond, shoulder length, and curly. She was neither short nor tall. Tex didn't think she'd ever be slender like a model; Melody was what Tex thought of as "luscious." Shaking his head, Tex put the picture back into his wallet for safe keeping.

He was nervous and confused. No woman had ever made him feel what Melody did. She soothed him, supported him, and wasn't afraid to call him on his bullshit. Tex had opened up more to her than anyone. She knew *him*, and that was scary as hell. She knew how he really felt about losing his leg. How he felt about the prosthetic. About being a SEAL. About his friends. She knew it all. A part of Tex was also hurt that Melody had cut him off so completely. They'd shared so much, and the fact that she could cut him out of her life so easily, was a blow.

Baby's head came up at Tex's feet as his phone vibrated and pinged with an incoming text message. The dog looked at him with her ears perked forward. Tex leaned down and smoothed his hand over her head. "It's probably Caroline or one of the girls wanting to make sure I arrived all right," he reassured the dog.

I'm scared

That's all the text said. Just those two words. Tex didn't recognize the number, but he immediately knew who it was. He sat up straight in his chair and quickly typed out a response. His heart was suddenly beating as quickly as if he'd just run a five mile race.

I know you are, Mel. Where are you?

Tex waited with bated breath for her response. He hoped like hell she'd text him back. He didn't know where her head was at, but if Melody admitted she was scared after almost two weeks of not talking to him at all, Tex knew it wasn't good. She was obviously skittish and Tex knew she could bolt at any time.

Nowhere

Cut the crap. Tell me where you are

Tex knew he had to get through to her. She was depressed and scared, not a good combination.

CA

WHERE exactly?

Anaheim

Keep going

What does it matter?

It matters to me. What hotel? What room?

What, are u going to come and get me?

Hotel? Room?

Holiday Inn Express. 305

Stay there. Don't move. Don't open the door to anyone. It's going to be OK

Tex didn't wait for her response. He knifed up out of the chair and grabbed Baby's leash. "Ready to go see mama, girl?" Baby whined in response, as if she knew exactly what was going on and where they were going.

Tex thanked God Melody had reached out to him. Tex headed to the garage where he'd parked his truck. He was going to get his girl. She wasn't alone anymore.

Chapter Four

MELODY PUT THE phone down and rested her head on her knees once again and closed her eyes. Stay put. She could do that. She could *so* do that. She didn't have the strength to go anywhere anyway. She was done. She had no idea what Tex had planned, but somehow she felt better knowing someone, other than her stalker, knew where she was.

She thought back to an online conversation she'd had with Tex not too long ago. She'd finally gotten up the courage to ask if he wanted to exchange pictures. She'd never forget his words. *I don't need a picture to know you're beautiful.*

Melody had laughed out loud then asked him what he meant, that she could weigh eight hundred pounds and be a shut-in for all he knew. He'd told her that her friendship and unconditional support meant everything to him and that he knew she had a beautiful soul. His words made her smile for days afterwards.

But now Melody wished she knew what Tex looked

like. She'd asked once and all he'd say was that he was a "washed up retired Navy guy who was missing half a leg." Melody didn't care if he was scarred, short, balding, or fat from eating too many doughnuts every day. He was her lifeline in this crazy new world she lived in. Melody knew he thought the loss of his leg was a deterrent for people getting close to him, but in her eyes, it made him who he was. And he was supportive, sensitive, and caring. Those things trumped physical looks in Melody's eyes any day.

But she couldn't help but picture Tex in her head as tall, dark, and handsome. He'd be taller than her, which wasn't hard since she was only five seven. He'd be big enough to envelop her in his arms and let her feel surrounded by his heat. She hadn't felt safe in so long, that alone would be heaven. He'd be muscular and strong, with bulging muscles, but not too bulky. His hair would be short, but still a bit too long to be military short, and his broad shoulders would be wide enough to… Melody stopped her thoughts with a jerk.

Whatever. All that stuff was crap. She didn't care if he didn't look like a man on the cover of a romance novel. She just needed *him*. His words and his strength. Melody had looked after herself for a long time now, and had done a pretty damn good job of it too. But it'd be nice to have some help.

Melody remembered that Tex's SEAL friends lived

in California. Maybe he'd call them and they would offer to help. That had to be it. She assumed Tex would text her back to let her know what he had planned. He'd said for her not to open her door. Melody laughed a bitter little laugh. Tex didn't have to tell her. She wasn't opening the door for anyone. She didn't feel safe sitting in the floor curled into a little ball, but it was better than wandering outside or opening the door for someone who may or may not be a stalker bent on hurting her. She knew that for a fact.

Melody closed her eyes and concentrated on breathing. Nothing else, just breathing in and out. She could forget… for just a moment… that someone wanted her dead and she was alone in the world.

TEX IGNORED THE dirty look he received from the front desk clerk as he walked as quickly as possible through the lobby to the elevator. He preferred the stairs, but his leg was still sore and he didn't want to push it any more than he already had. Tex knew he had to give it a rest soon, but until he made sure Melody was safe, he wasn't going to take the time.

Baby was silent at his side. Tex could tell she was tense, but she hadn't made a noise. Thank God the hotel was pet friendly, even if the clerk wasn't. The elevator opened at the third floor and Tex got out and followed the sign and headed down the hall toward room 305.

He paused outside the door and quickly sent Melody a text.

In a moment there will be a knock at your door. It's fine. Look through the peephole first.

Tex took a deep breath and reached down and picked Baby up. He knocked on the door with one hand and held the dog up so that her face was level with the peephole in the door. He could've just texted her and said he was there and to let him in, but wasn't sure she'd believe him. Tex knew of no other way to get Melody to trust him, to open the door, other than to show her Baby, her beloved dog. Of course it was also something a stalker might do, but Tex was hoping Mel would be so surprised and excited to see her dog, that she'd let him in. He'd remind her it wasn't smart after he was inside with her.

He waited, holding his breath, and suddenly the door was open.

The woman standing in front of Tex took his breath away. She seemed tired, and stressed, but other than the change in hair color, she looked just as she did in the photo Amy had given him. Tex had spent some time admiring Melody's photo, but he never would've imagined how cute she was in person.

Melody was about average height for a woman. She came up to about his chin. She had long brown hair that currently looked like it could use a good wash. She was wearing a pair of ragged jeans that probably should've been replaced a few years ago, but they looked well-worn and comfortable. She was wearing a simple T-shirt that showed nothing and everything at the same time. She was curvy. Tex didn't know sizes, he only knew what he liked, and he definitely liked what he was looking at. He hadn't really been able to see her curves in the picture of her standing next to Amy, but he approved.

Melody looked stressed, but healthy. He'd seen way too many women since he'd been in California that thought sexy meant starving yourself. Hell, he saw way too many women on his many missions that were scary underweight and would kill for the chance to eat enough to have the curves Melody had.

Her breasts strained against the shirt she was wearing and her hips flared out from her waist in a way that made Tex want to grab them and hold her against him. He would've stood there admiring her longer, but Baby was struggling to get out of his arms and he didn't want to drop her.

Tex set Baby on the ground and the dog leaped for Melody. Actually leaped. If Tex had any doubt in his mind that this *was* Melody, the dog had just obliterated them.

Mindful of the danger he swore he could actually feel in the air, Tex gently scooted the reunion out of the hallway and into Melody's room. He watched as dog and mistress jubilantly greeted each other after being apart for so long. Melody ended up sitting on the floor with the fifty pound coonhound in her lap frantically whining and licking the tears that coursed down her face.

"Baby! Oh my God, Baby. I can't believe you're here! I missed you so much."

Melody's words were halting and as heartfelt as any Tex had ever heard. He waited patiently, leaning up against the door, for Melody to notice him. It was the first time he'd ever been upstaged by a dog, but he loved every second of it.

Melody hugged her dog and buried her head in her scruff. She hadn't ever expected to see Baby again. The hardest part about leaving Pennsylvania had been leaving her dog. Melody had seen her on an online ad the shelter back home had run. Baby had been emaciated and covered in sores and fleas and ticks. Her sad eyes had sucked Melody in the first time she'd seen them looking at her through her computer screen.

Melody had dropped everything and gone to the shelter that afternoon. The employees told her that the dog had most likely been abused and was scared to death of people. She was set to be euthanized the next day, but the volunteers had wanted to try one more time to get her adopted. Melody had gone into the area where the dog pens were and almost cried when she'd seen Baby for the first time. She'd been huddled against the back wall of her enclosure and shivered uncontrollably. Melody had been allowed to go into the pen with her. It had taken thirty minutes, but Melody had patiently sat on the floor and talked to the dog. She murmured nonsense for every second of those thirty minutes.

Baby had eventually climbed into Melody's lap, all thirty-five underweight pounds of her, and shivered while Melody petted and cooed to her. Melody had taken her home that night and eventually Baby had come out of her shell. Melody knew she'd never be the most social dog, but they loved each other unconditionally.

The stalker had threatened to kill Baby though, which was why Melody left her behind in Pennsylvania. The note had said,

I hate animals. I'll cut off its head and leave it on a stick in your yard if you don't get rid of it.

Melody believed it. She'd woken up the next morning to find a headless squirrel on her front porch stuck into a flower pot on a skewer. It was a warning Melody took to heart. She'd arranged to take Baby to Amy's house the next day and had left Pennsylvania within the week, after dropping off her beloved dog with her best friend.

Melody looked up through her tears at the man standing inside her hotel room. He hadn't said a word throughout her reunion with Baby. For a second she was scared. Yes, he'd brought her Baby, but it could be the stalker. She was a day late and a dollar short in her thinking, of course. He might have used her dog to gain entry to her room. She was an idiot. Just as Melody started panicking, the man moved.

He leaned over and pulled up the left leg of his jeans, just enough that Melody could see the shiny medal of a prosthetic device.

"Tex," Melody breathed, hardly believing he was here. *Here.* Tex was here. She stood up, awkwardly, not knowing what to say.

"Come here, Mel."

Melody sighed in relief. She took a step toward Tex and suddenly she was in his arms. She wrapped her arms around the man, not exactly a stranger, but not exactly someone she knew, and cried.

She cried in relief for not being alone. She cried because he'd brought her Baby. She cried for being so scared for so long. Melody didn't feel Tex moving her backwards, but somehow she found herself sitting in

Tex's lap while he settled into the arm chair in the corner of the room.

"Shhhh, Mel. It's okay. I'm here. You're safe."

Not wanting to think about how awkward this should be, but somehow wasn't, and not wanting to think about anything else either, Melody buried her head in Tex's chest and held on to him even tighter.

Tex tightened his hold on the woman in his lap. His thoughts swung wildly from arousal, to sympathy, to joy that he was finally seeing, and holding the woman he'd slowly gotten to know over the past months. He'd be a liar if he hadn't thought about her in his arms at least once over the last half a year, but the reality was so much better.

Feeling the moment Melody got herself together, Tex waited. As much as he wanted to demand she tell him everything and scold her for not getting in touch with him sooner, he couldn't do it. He'd wait for her to be ready.

Melody took a deep breath. She had to get herself together. She picked her head up and looked around for Baby. She was sitting right at Tex's feet, just looking at the two of them. When she saw Melody looking at her, she leaned forward and put her head on the arm of the chair as her tail wagged rhythmically behind her. Melody reached out and petted the dog. "God, I missed you, Baby."

Baby whined and licked Melody's hand.

"That's enough, girl. Go lie down. I gotta talk to your mama." Tex's voice was affectionate, but stern at the same time.

Melody watched in amazement as her dog did what Tex told her to.

"How'd you get her to do that? I couldn't ever train her to do anything. Stubborn hound."

"Mel, look at me."

Tex's voice was low and rumbly and it made goosebumps rise up and down Melody's arms. He was... more than she expected. She'd told herself that she wouldn't care if he wasn't good looking, but lord. Seeing him in the flesh was overwhelming. He wasn't good looking... he was *good looking*. Melody couldn't feel an ounce of fat on him. Tex's thighs under her butt were rock hard. The chest she'd been lying against for the last ten minutes was also muscular and Melody would bet every dime she had that he had at least a six pack under his shirt. His dark hair was short at least she thought so, but it was his eyes that really struck her. They were a deep brown, and they looked at her as if she was the most important thing in the world. Tex didn't fidget. He didn't move. Melody knew he was looking right at her, waiting for her to meet his eyes.

She looked up. Yup. Those piercing eyes were focused on her.

"My name is John Keegan, but everyone calls me Tex. I'm thirty-five years old. I'm medically retired from the Navy. I was a Navy SEAL. My leg was injured in my last mission and they had to take half of it off. I have a prosthetic now. My stump isn't pretty. I've never had a pet, never really thought about it, but having spent the last four days or so with Baby, I'm a convert. I've been out of my mind with worry for you, Mel. I met Amy and her family. I drove three days straight across the country to get to you. I swear to you, I might not be whole anymore, but I'm your friend. I'm here to help you. We'll figure this out so you can get back to your life so you don't have to run or be scared anymore."

Melody knew her lip was quivering. She tried to hold her tears back. She'd cried way too much in the last day or so.

She followed his example, her voice low. "My name is Melody Grace. I'm twenty-seven. I eat too much crap and need to lose too many pounds to count. I'm a closed caption reporter, and I'm good at it. I can type one hundred words a minute with only a three percent error rate. In my spare time, when I was lonely, I used to surf the Internet for someone to talk to. I met someone a few months ago that I really liked." Melody looked down and felt Tex's hand at her chin, nudging it upward.

"Go on, Mel," Tex whispered.

"I have a dog, a stubborn dog that I love with all my heart. And I'm scared. I could use some help."

Tex leaned forward and Melody's heart rate increased. He kissed her on the forehead and brought his other hand up from her back to her face. He framed her face and kept his eyes locked on hers.

"You're not alone anymore, Mel. You reached out for me all those months ago, and I won't let you pull back. We'll figure this out and make you safe. Make Baby safe. Just don't cut me off like that again. Please. You have no idea what it did to me when I saw you'd deleted your account."

"I won't." The words were said with barely any audible tone to them, but Tex heard them anyway.

"How long has it been since you've gotten any sleep?"

"I don't know. What day is it?"

Tex swore. "Okay. I'll deal with that in a second. What happened today?"

"What do you mean?"

"What happened today to make you break your silence and text me? I know it had to be something. You haven't contacted me once via text... until today. What happened?"

Melody fidgeted. God, Tex was way too smart. She gestured toward the letter lying in the middle of the floor behind them. "He found me and hand delivered a note."

"Hand delivered?"

"Yeah, there wasn't a post mark and the front desk clerk gave it to me."

Tex's mind immediately kicked into gear. If the stalker knew where she was, they had to move quickly. Without tensing, he moved his hand and put it on the back of her neck and stroked her nape with his thumb. He didn't want to startle her, but he figured Melody was smart enough to know she wasn't in a good situation and needed to get out of there. Hell, she'd gotten in touch with him, she definitely knew she wasn't safe.

"Mel, you know I'm here to help you, right?" Tex waited for her to nod then continued. "You've done a hell of a job staying ahead of whoever this is." At her look of disbelief, Tex continued, "Seriously. You've done everything right. I have more resources available to me than the average person. That's why I was able to find you so quickly. But it's more than obvious that whoever this is isn't going to stop. I need to know if you'll let me help you. If you'll let me make some decisions for you. I need to make a plan, but I can't if I know you're going to fight me on every decision I make."

Melody looked at the man in front of her. Could she give up control to him? She wasn't the type of woman to let others do things for her. She didn't like to take handouts. Hell, she didn't even want to take out student loans when she went to college and had paid them back as soon as she could after she graduated. Could she let this man, this virtual stranger, take over?

"I…" She paused, then tried again. "I want to. I'm tired of running, of hiding. But I'm not that good at letting others help me."

"I know, Mel. Believe me, I know this. That's why I asked. But I'm begging you to trust me. Let me figure out who's doing this. Let me help you get back to your life."

When Tex put it that way, how could she refuse? Melody nodded wordlessly.

"Thank you. I swear to you, you won't regret it. Now, we need to pack you up and get out of here. We'll head down to Riverton and spend a few days with Wolf. Then we'll head back to Pennsylvania."

"No!"

Tex just quirked an eyebrow at her.

"It's just… go back to Pennsylvania? That's where it started. My friends… my family…"

"I know, Mel, but this needs to end. We need to be in a place where it *can* end. If that's where your stalker is from, it'll be easier to draw him out and finish it."

Melody nodded. "It makes sense, but—"

"I'll be there with you, Mel. I'm not going anywhere."

"But—"

"No buts."

"Would you let me finish?" Melody sighed in exasperation, smiling to let Tex know she wasn't really pissed, but that she was also serious.

"Sorry. I have a tendency to take over. Make sure you tell me when I'm doing it too often."

"I will. What I was *going* to say is that you must have a life. You can't just come back to Pennsylvania and spend all your time there. What if nothing happens? What if he waits until you're gone again?"

"You done?" Tex asked, completely serious. "Get it all out now. Then I'll respond."

"You're annoying. How did I not know you're this annoying while we were chatting all those months?"

Tex smiled at Melody this time and tightened the hold on the back of her neck for a moment before resuming his slow sweep of his thumb against the sensitive skin. "Because I'm charming and charismatic?"

Melody just shook her head. She loved the feel of his hand on her neck, ignoring the way her nipples peaked at the sensual feel of his thumb rubbing against her hairline, she got herself together and continued, getting it all out as he requested.

"What if he hurts Baby, or Amy, or someone else I care about? What if you get tired of being there and start to resent me? What if *you* get hurt? What if it never ends? I don't think I can live like this for the rest of my life."

Tex waited a beat after Melody had finished talking, making sure she was really done. His heart ached for her. He hadn't really understood how stalking could affect people, but seeing Mel now, scared and hurting, he was starting to get it.

"Mel, I'm retired. That means I get paid every month to do nothing if I want to. I have the means and the time to come home with you for as long as it takes. But it's not going to take forever. We need to move this back to where it started so it can end. Whoever this is won't like that you came home. Won't like that you came back home with *me*. Your friends will be safe, because you'll tell them everything. They'll be vigilant. I have connections. We'll set up security for anyone you want. We won't let Baby out of our sight."

"But what are you going to do?"

Tex sighed. He didn't like what he thought it would take. "We need to egg him on, Mel. We can't fight an invisible enemy. He needs to make a mistake."

"You want to make me bait." Melody watched as Tex grimaced.

"Want to? Fuck no. What I *want* is for you to be safe. I want you to be able to live where you want without having to worry about some asshole hurting you, your dog, or even your friends. I want to keep you as far away from whoever is doing this as possible. If I could, I'd lock you away so he couldn't ever find you. But that obviously hasn't worked so far, and I'd prefer to be able to take a walk down the street with you on my arm without having to worry about someone shooting either one of us. In order to get to that point, unfortunately, we have to go back to where it started. I need more information in order to figure this out. It pisses me off, and I guarantee I will hate every second of putting you in danger, but I have a gut feeling this is the only way to make it end." Tex paused for a moment, looking Mel straight in the eyes as he did it.

Melody's impression of Tex increased. It was obvious he didn't like having to put her in danger, but he wasn't hiding the truth from her.

Finally he continued, "Yeah, I fucking hate it, but hear this now, Mel, I'll be right there. He's not going to hurt you. And this *will* end. You won't have to live like this for the rest of your life. I'm going to pull every marker, and do whatever it takes to make you safe. Swear to God."

"Okay."

"Okay?"

"Yeah, okay. I know I can't keep running. I hate it. I was already contemplating going home even before I contacted you. I hate being away from my family and Amy. I hate being scared. I'd rather face this asshole face-to-face than deal with his notes scaring me to death."

Tex couldn't resist. He leaned toward her, bringing her head into him with the hand at the back of her neck. He put his forehead against hers. "You're one tough cookie, Melody Grace." Then Tex kissed her. It was light and brief. Lighter and briefer than he wanted it to be, but he didn't want to confuse Mel any more than she probably was. She had to be feeling gratitude toward him, but Tex didn't want that. He wanted more.

Putting her back from him and trying to ignore how good she felt in his lap, Tex moved his hands to her hips. "Okay, let's get going. I'll get the letter, you get your stuff, and we'll head back to my hotel and pick up Baby's and my things. Then we'll get to Wolf's house and figure out our next steps."

Melody slowly stood up and realized as Tex steadied her before sliding his hands away from her hips, how much she enjoyed his hands on her. She felt his touch to the marrow of her bones. It'd been so long since she'd been touched, and Tex's hands just felt right. Melody got herself together and headed over to pick up her bags that she'd packed earlier in preparation for fleeing the hotel and California.

She watched as Tex picked up the letter on the floor with a washcloth. Melody knew he was trying to preserve any fingerprints that might, by some miracle, still be on the paper. His jaw clenched as he read the words on the page, but he didn't say anything.

Melody looked over at Baby. She sat calmly by the door, her eyes moving from Melody to Tex. Melody knew she should probably be offended or hurt that her dog was looking to Tex as much as she looked to her, but Melody couldn't find it in her. Tex had brought Baby to her. He'd cared enough to drive across the country to find her. He was going to help her figure out who the hell hated her so much that he'd threaten to hurt her and the people she loved.

Melody couldn't wait to get out of this hotel room and out of Anaheim. As much as she was scared to be going home, she was also looking forward to it. It was time to get back to her life, her real life.

Chapter Five

TEX LOOKED OVER at Melody. She was sitting in the passenger seat in his truck and Baby was sitting between them, her head resting on Mel's lap. Mel had her head against the headrest of the truck and her fingers were idly running over Baby's head. Baby had her eyes closed and every now and then Tex could hear a soft snore coming from the dog.

He hadn't lied to Melody. He'd never been around dogs much in his life, but Baby was awesome. She was sensitive, low-maintenance, and surprisingly protective. He liked that.

Keeping his voice low, he told Melody, "I need to tell you about my friends before we get there. It's likely they'll be overly exuberant."

Without opening her eyes, Tex heard Mel's response. "Overly exuberant? What's that code for?"

"It's code for the women were happy to see me yesterday, but they'll be absolutely thrilled to see me with *you*. They think I'm too much of a hermit and probably see me as Quasimodo. They'll probably push us together and assume we're sleeping together. Caroline will probably put us both in the basement together for the night."

"Wow. Uh. Okay."

"And the men know about you. Well, they know what I knew yesterday. They'll be concerned about you and will probably act overbearing and alpha. But I've got your back. Just go with it and know that I'll do what's best for *you*, no matter what *they* want to do."

Tex looked over Mel and saw she'd turned her head and was looking at him. He couldn't read what she was thinking, but he continued, "They're very 'hands on,' Mel. The men'll touch you, not sexually, but they'll put their hands on you. Your back, your head, your neck. The women'll hug you. A lot. They'll also probably pry a bit too much for just meeting you, but it's what they do. If you don't want that, tell me now and I'll tell them to back off. If it becomes too much, let me know and again, I'll tell them to lay off. They're touchy. They can't help it."

"Will you tell me more about them? How they met each other? What they're like? What you had to do with helping them?"

"Their stories aren't pretty, Mel."

"But they ended up together, right?"

"Yeah, they're together."

"Then their stories are beautiful."

Tex took his hand off the steering wheel and brought it to Mel's face. He ran his knuckles down her cheek once, then turned his attention back to the road.

"Wolf met Caroline when the plane they were on was hijacked. He left on a mission and the bad guys found her and stole her again. I helped Wolf find where they'd taken her. Abe and Alabama's story is a bit more tame, but essentially she saved his life in a fire, they got together, Abe did something dumb and Alabama took off. I tried to help find her, but it's a lot easier to hide when you don't use any kind of electronics. Then there was Fiona."

Tex's voice cracked. Fiona's story was the most personal to him. He felt Baby turn in between them and she reached up and licked his face once. Tex laughed and gently shoved Baby's face away from him. "Ew, girl…"

Melody laughed, leaned over and hugged Baby and tugged her back into her lap.

"I told you some of this online, but anyway, the team went into Mexico to rescue a Senator's daughter who'd been kidnapped, and they unexpectedly found Fiona there too. She was doing okay, but after they got home and the guys were on a mission, she had a flashback and ran. I found her because she used Cookie's credit card, and I talked to her every day, every four hours, until Cookie could get home and get to her."

His voice trailed off and this time it was Mel who reached over to offer comfort. She put her hand on his thigh, but didn't say anything.

"Then Mozart and Summer. Mozart met her when he went up to Big Bear. She was working at the motel where he was staying. The person Mozart had been tracking abducted her and tortured her with the intent to kill her. Luckily, I was able to trace the cell phone of another young lady he'd kidnapped that night as well. They got there in time to save both women. I heard Elizabeth, the other woman who was rescued with Summer, wasn't dealing well with what had happened to her and moved to Texas. I need to make a point to see what I can find out about her…how she's doing.

"Anyway, Dude and Cheyenne have a similar story. Dude is an expert with explosives. He met Cheyenne when he was called to a grocery store to diffuse a bomb some bad guys strapped to her. Of course he defused it, but then relatives of the bad guys took Cheyenne and tried to kill her and an apartment building full of people."

Tex took a deep breath and finished quickly. "Last there's Benny and Jessyka. She had a horrible ex who the guys took care of, but in order to get revenge he attacked Benny and lured Jessyka into his clutches. Even with her limp, she managed to save Benny's life. It would've been tough to find Benny without Jess leading me right to him."

"Leading you to him?"

Tex sighed. He knew this was coming. "This is going to sound bad, especially with what you're going through. But hear me out. Okay?"

"Ooo-kay."

Tex could hear the trepidation in her voice, but he continued on. It was going to come out sooner or later, so he might as well get it out in the open.

"My friends asked me to track their women. I made some GPS devices and sent them to the guys. They put them in earrings, their women's watches. Shoes. Clothes. I don't blame them one bit. Each one of them had been taken from them. None of us wanted it to happen again."

There was silence in the cab of the truck for a while. Tex let Mel think through what he said.

Finally she spoke. "It's not the same."

"What?"

"It's not the same. Your friends are doing it out of love. It's not the same."

Tex silently sighed in relief. He didn't think Melody would've freaked out, but he wasn't a hundred percent sure. "You're right, Mel. It's not. I'm the only one who receives the signals. The guys have the ability, but they trust me to keep the data. We've only needed to use it once, with Jessyka. She only let herself get taken because she knew Benny wasn't tracked and she was. She knew I'd know something was wrong."

"Can I have one?"

"What?" Tex couldn't believe he'd heard her right.

In a lower voice than she'd used before, Melody asked again, a little hesitantly, "Can you put one on me? I don't know what this guy wants. What if he takes me? You can find me if I have one of your tracking things right? You'll come and get me?"

Tex couldn't stand it. The tremble in her voice, the uncertainty, the vulnerability. He pulled the truck over to the side of the road and put it in park. Tex turned sideways in the seat and reached his hand out to Melody. He put it on the side of her head and held her eyes.

"I'd love to tell you that it'll never happen, Mel. But, unfortunately, I know more than anyone, that it can. I'll do everything possible to keep you safe, but sometimes it's not enough. So yes, if you want, I'll give you a tracker so if your stalker kidnaps you, I can find you. Whatever happens, don't you give up. If he finds you and takes you from me, do not egg this asshole on. Don't give him a reason to hurt or kill you. No matter what happens, we can get through it. Just remember that I'll be coming after you and I'll track you down. And I will, Mel. I will find you, you just have to give me the time to do it. Okay?"

Melody nodded. She knew asking to be tracked was weak, but she felt weak at the moment. Just him saying the words made her feel better. Made her feel more secure knowing someone, other than her stalker, would know where she was at all times. Someone she trusted. And she trusted Tex. She'd gotten to know him over the last six months they'd talked online. Hell, she knew him better than some of the people she'd grown up and went to school with. She knew him and, more importantly, she trusted him.

"Thank you for being honest with me. I know he's going to find me and it's just a matter of time before he catches up with me. Thank you for not pretending he won't. I swear, I won't give up. If he gets me, I'll hang on and wait for you to get to me."

Not addressing her pessimistic attitude, knowing there was a distinct possibility that she *could* get taken by her stalker, Tex said instead, "You're welcome. You okay? You need to stop? You hungry?"

Melody shook her head. "I'm okay. Even though they'll intimidate the hell out of me, I'm looking forward to meeting your friends."

"Don't feel intimidated, Mel. They're just like you. The women are strong and kick-ass and don't take any crap from their men. And my friends, they'll take one look at you and you'll be firmly in their 'you must be protected' camp."

"I'm not strong, Tex."

"The hell you aren't."

"I think I'm glad you see me that way."

"You'll see yourself that way too. Promise."

"Okay."

"Okay." Tex pulled Melody closer to him, ignoring the grunt of disapproval coming from Baby who was being mushed between them, and kissed her cheek. He pulled back and nodded at Mel. "Strong and kick-ass, Mel."

Tex then put the truck back in drive and pulled back onto the highway.

"BREATHE."

Melody tried, she did, but she was really nervous about meeting Tex's friends. The women all sounded awesome, and the men just plain freaked her out. She wasn't really ready for this, but she knew these people were as close to family as Tex had and she wanted to make a good impression.

"I'm okay."

"They're going to love you."

Melody could only nod as Tex got out of the truck and walked around to her side. He helped her out and Baby jumped down after her. Melody held the leash tightly as Tex reached for her hand. Melody jumped at the chance to grab hold.

They walked up to the house and the door opened as they reached it. A large man stood there and Melody could hear the voices of many others behind him. He stepped forward and mostly closed the door behind him.

"Tex. Melody. Glad you made it back so soon."

"Wolf." Tex gave him a chin lift. "Are they all in there?"

"Every last one."

Tex smiled at that. Of course everyone was here. "It okay if we stay here tonight?"

"Hell, Tex, as if Caroline would let you stay anywhere else." Wolf turned to Melody and held out his hand. "Melody, I'm Wolf. It's great to meet you. I'm glad Tex found you, but I had no doubt that he would. He's that good. Please know you're welcome to stay here as long as you want."

Melody took Wolf's hand in hers and shook it. "Thanks, but I go where Tex goes."

Wolf nodded as if he expected the answer. "I'm gonna say this quickly because if I know my wife, she'll be out here before not too much longer. You have my protection, Melody. You have my team's protection. Whatever you need, you've got it. Tex is a good man, he'll keep you safe, but if you need us, if Tex needs us, we're there. Understand?"

Melody could only nod. No words would come out.

Yesterday she'd been alone. Today she had a whole team of bad-ass SEALs at her back. It was hard to wrap her mind around.

At her side, Baby growled low. Melody realized Wolf still held her hand in his. She quickly dropped it and Baby moved in front of her, pushing Wolf back.

"Nice guard dog you got there."

"She's not a guard dog."

"Maybe not for anyone else, but she did the same thing when Tex was here before and Ice rushed him to give him a hug."

Melody turned to Tex. "Really?"

"Yeah, really."

Melody crouched down in front of Baby and whispered, "Good girl."

The men above her just laughed.

"Come on, Mel, let's get this over with."

Wolf laughed at the mock resignation in Tex's voice.

Tex held out a hand to Mel and helped her up. He put his arm around her waist and they followed Wolf into the house.

Melody could tell Tex was tired, because he was limping more than she'd noticed since meeting him. She remembered him telling her in one of their online conversations that when he overdid it, his limp would become more pronounced.

Before she could say anything, they entered a living room full of people.

"Tex is here!" One woman shouted and stood up quickly, and everyone in the room followed suit.

"Easy, Baby," Melody heard Tex say beside her. She looked down to see the scruff on the back of her dog's neck standing on end.

"You have to be Melody," another woman said a tad more calmly. "I'm Summer. I'm sure Tex has probably told you about all of us, but instead of using all their *real* names, he's probably only used their nicknames." She rolled her eyes and Melody smirked.

"Okay, so you met Wolf at the door." She pointed to each of the other men in the room and introduced them in succession. "Abe, Mozart, Dude, Benny, and Cookie."

"Wow, Summer, I'm impressed you know our nicknames," Cookie joked with her.

"Shut up, Hunter. Of course I know your nicknames. It's not like you guys will stop using them."

Melody just watched the by-play between everyone with amusement. She knew if she spent more time with this group of people she'd probably love them. They reminded her of her and Amy. A little goofy, a lot sarcastic, and funny to boot.

"Hi," Melody said shyly.

"Come sit over here by us. We can't wait to get to

know you better!"

Melody looked away from Summer, and turned to Tex. Before she could say anything, Tex leaned down to her to whisper into her ear. "It's okay, Mel. I'll be in the other room with the guys if you need me."

Melody nodded. "Okay."

Before she knew it, she was sitting in the middle of the six other women, Baby at her feet, laughing at the stories they shared about their men. Through the stories the women told, Melody could hear the love that came through. These women adored their men, and it was one hundred percent reciprocal.

"So Melody, tell us about Tex." It was Fiona that asked.

"What about him?"

"How'd you guys meet?"

"Well, I just met him face-to-face today."

"Wow! That's kinda cool! We just met him in person this morning. Well, Caroline had met him before, but not the rest of us," Jessyka shared. "Isn't he the *best*?"

Melody smiled at the affection in Jessyka's voice. "Yeah, he is."

"So? Deets woman!" Caroline demanded teasingly.

"We met online. I was bored and went into a chat room one night. He messaged me, and we started talking." Melody stopped, and got serious, remembering all that the women had been through. "He was so worried about you guys. Fiona, I interrupted him when he was trying to help you and he was so concerned about you." Melody turned to Jessyka. "He was pissed at you, Jess, but so proud that you'd risked yourself for Benny. You're all so lucky to have him." She stopped before she burst into tears. She normally wasn't quick to cry, but the stress over the last few months was catching up with her with a vengeance.

Fiona got out of her chair and came over to kneel in front of Melody and put her hands on her knees. "We love Tex. He means more to us than you'll ever know. We don't take him for granted and we're so thrilled he's here. We've been wanting to meet him forever. Take good care of him for us."

"I... we... we aren't together like that."

"If the look in either of your eyes is any indication, you will be soon."

Melody didn't know what to say. She just looked at Fiona, then around at the other women. They all had something in common. They were with hardcore SEALs that would give their lives for their women. Melody wanted that. She hadn't admitted it to herself until now, but she wanted it.

They all turned as the men came into the room. Melody could see furrowed lines in Tex's forehead and his pronounced limp made it obvious he was in pain.

Ignoring everyone else around her, Melody stood up and went straight to Tex. Baby trailed after her, close on her heels. Thinking quickly, not wanting to embarrass him in front of everyone, Melody said to him, but loud enough for everyone to hear, "I'm tired, Tex."

Tex knew what she'd done, knew she was lying so he could get off his feet, but didn't call her on it. He wouldn't mind getting more one-on-one time with Mel, and he knew the girls could talk all night if given half a chance. Melody's words were the impetus to clear the room. Slowly everyone came over to say their good-byes to both Tex and Melody and Caroline and Wolf.

Cheyenne gave her a quick hug and stepped aside for her man. Dude put his hand under Melody's chin and lifted her head until she had no choice but to look him in the eyes.

"You might not know this, but you managed to hook up with the right man. Tex will do what it takes to make sure you're safe. He can do some amazing shit on the computer. We've all relied on him, the government relies on him, and I know for a fact there are several top-secret military groups out there who rely on him. But most importantly, you can trust him, Melody. We've got his, and your, back, but when push comes to shove, trust Tex."

Melody could only nod as she gazed up at the intense man in front of her. His words were more of a command than anything else and Mel almost felt compelled to agree with him. If it wasn't for Cheyenne standing next to him with a hand on his arm and smiling huge, she probably would've been worried. He had a way about him that Mel didn't get from the others. More…take-charge. That wasn't exactly the word she was looking for, but before she could think too much about it, Dude leaned down and gave her a brief kiss on the cheek before stepping back so the others could approach her and say their good-byes as well.

Melody got a hug from everyone before they left, along with more reassurances that she'd be safe with Tex. She was basically passed from one person to the next until there were only four of them left. Tex had been right. His friends were touchy, but Melody liked it. They were affectionate and it was obvious they cared about Tex.

"I've got the room all set up for you guys. Melody, I got Baby's food from the car and it's downstairs for you to feed her in the morning. Your bags are also down in the basement. If there's anything you need, just either let us know or help yourself. Tex, you know the drill."

Tex nodded at Wolf. "Thanks, man. Appreciate it."

"See you in the morning."

Tex turned and headed for the basement door. Baby, once again, put herself at his side as they began to head down the stairs. He had to let go of Mel and he limped down the stairs. Tex quickly tried to think about how this would work. He knew the bed was only a queen. It should be big enough for them, but he didn't know what Mel would think about it. He'd told her in the car that Caroline would probably put them in the basement room together. But most people would probably see this as very odd… them just meeting today and tonight sleeping in the same bed, but Tex felt as if he knew Melody a hundred times better than most of the women he'd slept with in the past.

More importantly was the issue of his prosthesis. He didn't want her to see his stump, but there was no way he could sleep in it. His leg was on fire. He needed to rub it down and give it a break from the confines of the prosthetic.

"If it's okay, I'll go first in the bathroom," Tex tried to be nonchalant.

"No problem." Melody watched as Tex limped into the small room. She couldn't quite read his mood. Hell, she didn't really know him, no wonder she couldn't read him. They did really well talking to each other on the computer, but in person it was different.

Melody looked around. There was a bed in the middle of the room with a dresser against a wall. Around a corner there was a small kitchenette that held a small refrigerator and a sink. There was a coffee maker on the counter and a little two-seater table with chairs tucked underneath.

She knew she should probably be asking Caroline if there was another room she could stay in. Sleeping in the same bed with Tex after only meeting him a few hours ago was insane. But it'd been so long since she'd felt safe, Melody couldn't bring herself to care. She knew Tex. Knew he was a kick-ass SEAL and that he could hurt her a million different ways, but she also knew he was insecure. He'd go out of his way to make her feel comfortable and he'd never ever hurt her. Maybe she was being naïve believing that, but after meeting Wolf and the other SEALs who obviously respected and admired Tex, and after hearing from the women he'd had a hand in saving, she knew she was safe, and that there was nowhere she'd rather be, than right by his side.

She turned toward the bathroom door and tilted her head. What was going through Tex's head? Baby jumped up on the bed and turned in circles at the foot. Melody smiled. It was obvious she'd been here before.

Melody looked back as the bathroom door opened behind her. Tex limped out wearing a tattered T-shirt and a pair of cut-off sweatpants which hung low on his hips. Melody gulped. She remembered thinking she wouldn't care if Tex had turned out to be overweight, and she wouldn't have, but he was gorgeous. Any woman who would turn him down because of his leg was obviously certifiably insane.

"It's all yours. Take your time."

Melody looked critically at Tex. Thinking about his personality and what she knew of him, something seemed off. She thought about it a bit more and it came to her.

"You don't have to be embarrassed about your leg with me."

Tex froze and turned to Melody, but didn't say anything.

"Seriously. I remember you told me how your leg would hurt when you wore your prosthetic all day. You told me how you had to massage it for it to feel better. I know about the phantom pains, Tex. You're in pain, I can see it. Please don't be embarrassed around me."

"It's not pretty, Mel."

"I didn't expect it would be."

Tex looked at Mel and struggled with himself. He didn't want to show her his leg. It was the last thing he wanted to do. He wanted to impress her, and he didn't think seeing his scarred leg would. He hated feeling like this, it went against everything he was, but the feeling was there and wouldn't leave.

"Trust me. I'm putting my life in your hands. Trust me not to let you down here," Melody whispered, not moving. When Tex nodded, she said, trying to be no-nonsense about it, "Okay, take off those pants and get on the bed. But don't take it off yet. I want to see how it works."

"Now who's bossy?"

Tex smiled as he said it, but Melody could see it didn't reach his eyes. She didn't push it, but turned to go into the bathroom, giving Tex some time to get comfortable without her around watching him. She hurried through her nightly routine, glad Wolf had the foresight to bring her bag downstairs, and went back into the bedroom. She'd changed into a long T-shirt and a pair of boxer shorts.

Tex had turned the lights down and he was sitting on the bed propped up by the pillows behind him. He'd removed his sweatpants and was in a pair of boxer shorts. Melody walked over to the bed and climbed on.

"Jesus, Tex, I know you're nervous as hell and you really *really* don't want to share this with me, but you are sex on a fucking stick. Seriously."

"Mel—"

"No, Tex. Look at you." Melody ran her eyes over the man lying next to her. "I'm so not in your league at all. I wish I had x-ray vision because I bet you have a six-pack under that shirt. Your arms are muscular as all hell and your legs? Damn. I'll never see another pair of boxers and not be able to recall this moment right here. You've been concerned all this time about how a woman would react when she sees your leg? I can tell you right now that they wouldn't even care. They'd be too busy looking at the rest of you because it is fiiiiine."

Tex burst out laughing. He'd been afraid Mel would be disgusted by his leg. He should've known better. Her words gave him back some of the self-esteem that had slowly eroded over the years since he'd been injured. "Mel, look at me."

Melody waved her hand at him, refusing to look away from his body. "Sorry, busy at the moment." She said it with a smile, still checking him out.

Tex grasped Mel's chin in his hand and gently turned her head toward him. "Thank you, Mel. And you're wrong, You're definitely in my league."

"I'm not, and it's fine."

Tex tightened the hold he had on her face when she tried to turn away. "No, look at me. You want to know what I thought the first time I saw you standing in that hotel room?"

"Not particularly."

Tex ignored her and continued. "I thought to myself that it was no wonder someone has become obsessed with you. A horrible thought, but true none-the-less."

Melody looked at Tex in bewilderment, her brows wrinkling in confusion.

"Yeah, you're beautiful."

"I'm not."

"Okay, to me you're not just beautiful, you're gorgeous. Your body is perfect."

"You haven't seen me, Tex. I'm far from gorgeous."

"You're wrong. I see you. You said you'll never see a pair of boxers the same way again? The same goes for me. You're lush. Men love that. They *want* that. The entertainment world tries to shove stick-figured women down our throats as the ideal woman, but they couldn't be further from the truth. Your curves are to die for. I know you probably don't feel that way, women never understand these things. But Mel, honestly, we don't want skin and bones, and muscular looks good on television and in magazines, but it feels so much better to have soft skin surrounding us than hard angles and muscles. We like soft, Mel. *I* like soft."

Melody knew she was breathing too hard, but she couldn't take her eyes away from Tex. His words slid over her like a warm blanket just taken from a dryer.

"If after you see me, all of me, you're still interested, Mel, I'm yours. I like you. I've gotten to know you over the last six months and I like what I've gotten to know. Seeing you? Feeling the chemistry between us? Fucking perfect. Yeah. I want you."

"It's only been a day," Melody whispered uncertainly, not really believing her own words.

"It hasn't only been a day and you know it. We started this six months ago. I'm not the kind of guy who chats with a woman every day for six months, Mel.

Maybe a day or two, but not six months. We might have *seen* each other for the first time today, but I've known you for half a year. You think I would've come after you if it wasn't more?"

"Maybe. You're a SEAL, Tex. It's what you do."

"Bullshit. Yeah, I might have once rescued people for a living, but I'm retired now. I haven't suddenly dropped everything to go traipsing off around the country looking for random missing people. But the second *you* canceled your account online, I was trying to figure out how to find and get to you."

Tex dropped his hand from Melody's face and gestured to his leg with his chin as if to change the subject and tell her to get on with it.

Without a word, but with Tex's words tumbling around in her brain, Mel turned her attention to his leg. She said briskly, trying to hide how much his words confused, excited, and aroused her all at the same time, "Okay, show me how this thing works."

"I have what's known as a transfemoral amputation, meaning an amputation above the knee. The prosthetic is held in place by suction, so I don't need any other type of suspension to keep it in place. It fits snugly onto what's left of my leg and the airtight seal keeps it from slipping out."

"How do you break the seal to get it off?"

"The type of liner I have is a seal-in liner. It creates a

strong, airtight seal which allows a good fit and it comes with a button that if you push it, it breaks the seal."

Melody couldn't prevent the little giggle that escaped and the inappropriate comment which spewed from her mouth. "You have a magic button."

Tex grinned at her. Jesus, she was cute. He couldn't stop the innuendo from coming out of his mouth if his life depended on it. "Yeah, Mel, now we both have a magic button." She blushed, as he knew she would, and he laughed, but sobered quickly, knowing what she was about to see. "It's not pretty, Mel. But if you're gonna do it, get it over with."

Melody reached out and pressed the button that Tex had shown her. The suction on the device was broken and it popped right off into her hands.

Working quickly, so as not to prolong any embarrassment he might have over what she was doing, Melody lifted the prosthetic leg and leaned over and placed it on the floor behind her. She turned back around to see Tex pulling the sleeve off his stump that served as the liner for the prosthetic.

He was right, the skin around his leg wasn't pretty. It was red and swollen and Melody winced in sympathy.

"Jeez, Tex. That looks like it's really painful. Do you have any lotion or something?"

"Yeah, I'm supposed to use it every night, but I haven't really taken it off much in the last week."

"Where is it?"

Without a word, Tex leaned over to the nightstand and grabbed a small bottle that Melody had missed. He'd obviously gotten it ready to go while she'd been in the bathroom.

Melody took it out of his hand and rubbed a large dollop of the eucalyptus smelling lotion between her hands then leaned over his leg.

Tex grabbed her wrist before she could touch him. "You don't have to do this. I can do it."

"I want to. Please."

Tex sat back and closed his eyes and braced.

Chapter Six

MELODY REFUSED TO let the tears gathering in her eyes fall. She watched as Tex leaned back and closed his eyes. She looked back at what was left of his leg. Where his leg had been removed were scars crisscrossing it and it looked beyond painful. She rubbed her hands together warming the lotion before she put her hands on Tex's leg.

She massaged and rubbed the stump, making sure to rub the creamy soothing lotion into all parts of his leg. She moved her way up to his thigh, trying to rub out the sore muscles. Finally, she sat back and climbed off the bed.

She went into the bathroom and washed her hands, then came back into the room. Tex had gotten under the covers. Melody turned off the light on the side of the bed and climbed into the other side. She lay on her back for a moment. She knew Tex would be a gentleman and wouldn't make the first move.

She turned on her side and scooted over to Tex's

side. She put one arm over his chest and laid her head on his shoulder as if she did it every night.

"Thank you," Melody whispered.

Tex shifted until one arm could curl around Mel's shoulder and whispered back, "No, thank *you*."

Melody lay in bed for a long while, listening to Tex's breathing slow, then even out in the cadence of sleep. Once she knew he was asleep, she finally let the tears fall. She wept silently for the brave soldier Tex had been and for what he now was going through. From their many online conversations she knew he was still very sensitive about his disability and hated to bring attention to it. She also knew how painful it still was.

Finally the tears eased and Melody snuggled further into Tex's side. She sighed in bliss when his arm tightened around her for a moment and he murmured sleepily, not really awake, but not really asleep.

"Sleep, Mel."

"Okay," she whispered back. She closed her eyes and within moments was out. It was the first time in a long time she felt safe as she slept.

The next morning, Melody stirred when she heard Caroline call out from the vicinity of the stairs, "Good morning!"

She looked down and saw that she and Tex had thrown the covers off of themselves during the night, probably because their shared body heat made the blankets unnecessary, and Tex's stump was exposed. Melody saw the look of panic on his face at the thought of Caroline seeing him without his prosthetic. Without thinking, just wanting to protect Tex, Melody reached down to grab the blanket and pulled it up to their waists just as Caroline poked her head around the corner of the room.

"Morning, you two! I figured you'd want to get an early start this morning so I'm your wakeup call. I'll have breakfast ready for you when you get upstairs. Don't dawdle." Then she disappeared from view and Melody heard her heading back up the stairs.

Without looking at Tex, Melody went to scoot out of bed when she felt Tex's hand on her arm. She gestured at the bathroom, "I'm just going to—"

Her words were cut off when Tex pulled on her arm until she was lying back on the bed with him looming over her. "Why'd you do that?"

Knowing what he meant, Melody answered honestly, "Because I know it makes you uncomfortable for anyone to see your leg." Melody fidgeted as Tex continued to look down at her. "Should I—"

"Hush."

When Tex didn't say anything else, but continued to look down at her, Melody tried again. "Tex, I—"

"You didn't flinch. I watched and last night, you saw my leg and you didn't even flinch. You massaged it, you worked the kinks out of my thigh, you kept Ice from seeing it. You, looking like you do, draping yourself over my chest last night, being sweetly shy. I told you if you could stomach what you saw, that I'd be yours if you wanted me. Well, I'm telling you Mel, I'm yours."

Melody tried again. "Tex—"

He interrupted her again. "I haven't trusted anyone other than my doctors to see my leg since it happened. Not even the guys. No one. Just you."

"Would you stop interrupting me!" Melody huffed out irritably, but secretly pleased Tex had allowed her to see his leg when he hadn't even shown it to his friends.

Tex grinned down at her and acknowledged, not very apologetically, "Sorry."

"I have no idea why you're self-conscious about your leg. Yeah, you hurt it. Yeah, you limp a bit. Yeah, it looks painful. But you, Tex, you're amazing. You're more than your leg. I like you. I liked you before we met. I didn't talk to anyone else while I was hiding out. Only you. I hated to leave you waiting for me in that chat room. All that had *nothing* to do with your leg. It's *you*. Your friends won't care about your leg. They won't pity you, they won't think bad about you. They love you. You're confusing as hell. One minute I want to smack you, and the next I want to kiss you. You say stuff I don't get. And I don't know what it means when you say you're mine."

Still smiling, thinking her outburst was adorable, Tex told her, "It means whatever you want it to mean, Mel. We have a long drive ahead of us. We have to figure out who's stalking you. You need to get your life figured out. But I hope somewhere in there we can make time to get to know each other even better in real life instead of only on the computer. Somewhere along the line I hope you can decide if you *want* me to be yours."

"Okay, Tex." Melody knew she'd say anything to get away and have a second to think about what he'd just told her.

Seeing the confusion on her face and having pity on her, Tex told her, "Okay, Mel. Go on, get ready to go. I'll shower after you."

"Do you need help with—"

As usual, Tex cut her off and said with only a hint of sarcasm, "I've got it. I've been doing it on my own for a while now."

"But I'm here. I can help you. I *want* to help you."

"Not today. Last night was hard enough for me. Let me get used to it."

Melody shook her head. "All right, but if you're going to be mine, you have to let me help you sooner or later."

"Deal."

"Seriously you have to... wait... what?"

"I'm going to kiss you before I let you up to shower."

Melody's brain stuttered to a halt. He changed topics so quickly she was having a hard time keeping up, but a kiss? She'd been dreaming about him kissing her, *really* kissing her, since she'd met him standing in her hotel room. Hell, before that. She'd never admit, even under torture, that she'd gone to sleep more than once dreaming of the wonderful man she'd been chatting with online.

"Did you hear me, Mel?"

"Uh huh."

Tex grinned. "Fuck, you're cute when you're befuddled." Then he leaned down and took her mouth with his own. He supposed he should've kept it light and sweet, but he didn't feel light and sweet. He felt raw and exposed, and the chemistry they'd been dancing around for the last day exploded when his lips touched hers.

Melody slanted her head to improve the angle of their kiss. Her hands came up to grasp at his sides. Tex drove his tongue into Melody's mouth and stroked. He licked over her lips then plunged back inside. He mimicked what it might be like when they made love, because he knew they'd eventually end up doing more than just sleeping when they shared a bed.

Tex almost lost it when Melody captured his tongue

and sucked on it, closing her lips around it and caressing it with her own tongue in the process. He lifted his head and stared down at Melody.

"Fuck, woman."

Melody smiled up at him and licked her lips. She flattened her hands at his waist and ran them up and down slowly. "That was… yeah… uh… wow."

Tex's mouth quirked into a grin. "Yeah. Wow. Thank you for looking out for me."

"You're welcome."

Rolling over and sitting up, Tex said, "Now, go shower. I'll take Baby out while you get ready."

Melody laughed. She'd forgotten all about her dog, who was still curled into a ball at the foot of the bed, watching them. "Okay, Tex. Whatever you say." She got up off the bed, snooter kissed Baby, and walked into the bathroom, managing not to look back at the sexy-as-hell man sitting on the bed.

Chapter Seven

"**W**ANNA PLAY A game?" Melody asked Tex. It was the day after they'd left California and she was bored. The first day was exciting, just because it was different. When she'd fled Pennsylvania, she'd rented a car with cash she'd pulled out of her bank account and driven across the country, but somehow this was different. She wasn't as scared and since Tex had done most of the driving so far, she could watch the ever-changing countryside as it went by.

They'd stopped somewhere in eastern New Mexico the first night of their trip. Melody thought it would be awkward when they stopped, but Tex made it easier than she thought it could be.

He asked her to stay in the car while he checked in. He'd told her that while it might be a bit awkward to stay in the same room, he didn't want to leave her alone, even if she was just next door. Melody agreed without reservation, after all, they'd spent the night before in each other's arms and they weren't strangers. Besides that, she felt safe with Tex. She didn't want to be in a room by herself. She wanted to be with Tex.

Tex had gotten a room with two queen beds, not wanting to push Mel into anything she wasn't ready for, but when push came to shove, Melody had asked if she could sleep in the same bed as him. He'd agreed and after she'd once again massaged his leg and stump, they'd settled into each other arms.

Just as she'd been drifting off to sleep, Tex said in a low voice, "I hate traveling." Melody was instantly awake.

"Why?"

"Because without my prosthetic, I'm vulnerable. If something happens in the middle of the night, I can't jump up and deal with it like I used to be able to. Whether it's a knock on the door, someone trying to break in, a fire, or whatever. I'm stuck in bed until I can get my leg on. I hate it."

Melody wasn't sure what to say. She hadn't thought about it, but now that he put the images in her head, they wouldn't leave. "You're the least vulnerable man I've ever met." She put every ounce of conviction into her voice as she could.

"You don't have to—"

Melody interrupted him. "I'm not." She felt movement under her cheek and lifted her head to see he was laughing.

"You don't even know what I was going to say."

"Don't care. Whatever it was, was going to be crap. You could probably break someone in half if they broke in here. You could hop to the door and down the hall and outrun any fire that dared to try to burn you. If someone knocked, you could have your leg strapped on before they got any words out. In fact..." Melody pushed herself up even more and peered down at Tex in the dark room. "I bet you've practiced getting your leg on as fast as you can... haven't you?"

When he grinned sheepishly up at her, Melody smiled back and brought her hands up to tickle his sides. "How long? What's your fastest time?"

She let out a girly shriek when he flipped her over and trapped her hands in one of his above her head.

"There I was, getting all touchy feely with you and you had to go and ruin it." His words were said with a smile and a twinkle in his eye, but Melody still immediately felt bad.

"Seriously, Tex, I'm sorry you feel that way, but if I had my pick between all your friends and you, as to who would be with me in this hotel room right now, I'd still pick you. *You* make me feel safe. Two legs, one arm, no legs, no arms. I'd still pick you."

Without a word, Tex leaned down and kissed Melody deeply and with all the emotion he couldn't figure out how to put into words. Her trust meant the world to him. Since his surgery, he'd always felt somehow less than his other SEAL friends. Two sentences was all it took to bring back his self-esteem.

Not letting the kiss morph into anything more, it still seemed too soon, Tex turned again until they'd resumed their earlier positions. Throughout everything, Baby hadn't moved, she just slept, snoring softly, at the end of the bed in a super-ball.

When they'd settled down, and just as Melody was slipping back into sleep, she heard Tex whisper, "Twenty three seconds."

Melody merely smiled, turned her head and kissed his chest, and laid her cheek back down without a word. She'd known in her gut he'd practiced putting his prosthetic on.

Now it was four hours into another long driving day and Melody was bored.

"What kind of game did you have in mind?" Tex asked, briefly looking over at Melody.

"Well, it's not a game per se, but more of an information sharing thing. I'll tell you something interesting about me, and then you do the same."

Expecting an argument, Melody was surprised when Tex agreed immediately. "Sure. You go first."

Melody looked down at Baby who was sleeping between them in the truck. She'd been an excellent traveling companion. Melody had never traveled for as many hours on the road as this with her before, but it didn't really surprise her. Baby had always been reticent and quiet and eager to please. Melody supposed that had to do with whatever she went through before she ended up in the shelter. Melody ran her hand down her dog's head and back. Baby didn't move, but groaned in her sleep. Melody smiled.

"Growing up, I was a cat person. My parents had cats and I always knew when I grew up I was going to have a household full of cats too."

"What happened?"

"I got busy, didn't think it was fair to have a pet when I was busy all the time. Then I saw Baby's picture in an online ad the shelter had run and they'd said she would be euthanized the next day if she didn't get adopted. Something about her face tugged at my heartstrings and I went right down to the shelter."

"She was lucky."

"No," Melody countered, "I'm the lucky one. Baby is the best dog I could've asked for. It killed me to leave her behind when I left Pennsylvania, but I knew it'd be even worse if my stalker got a hold of her and killed her. I don't know what I'd do without her."

After a comfortable silence, Melody prodded Tex, "Your turn."

"I almost didn't message you that first night."

"Really? Why did you change your mind?"

"Well, there was someone calling herself Busty Betty who I messaged first. She didn't answer."

"So I was your second choice?" Melody looked over at Tex and saw he was trying to hide a grin. She smacked him in the arm. "You jerk. You're lying aren't you?"

Tex lost his battle with hiding his smile and laughed out loud. "Yeah, I was honest about almost not messaging you, but something told me it'd be worth my while."

"And was it?"

"Hell yeah. Best fucking decision I've made in my entire life." Tex glanced over at Mel so she'd know he was completely serious.

"I'm glad you did."

"Me too. Okay, your turn again."

"My second toe is longer than my big toe."

Tex laughed out loud. He hadn't realized how little he laughed until Mel came into his life. "I'll have to check that out for myself." He thought for a moment, then continued the game. "I can't stand bananas."

"Bananas?"

"Yeah, weird huh? I don't know if it's the consistency of the fruit or something. I just can't choke it down."

"What about banana flavored candy?" Mel asked curiously.

"Nope."

"That's weird."

"Hey!"

Melody chuckled. "Sorry, but it is." She continued on with the game. "My secret obsession is watching COPS."

"Please tell me you're kidding."

Giggling, Melody admitted, "Nope. Love it. People can be such idiots, and I especially love it when the police officers laugh at the criminals."

"I have an admission," Tex told her.

"Yeah?"

"I've never seen an episode of COPS."

"Oh my God! We are so finding one tonight when we get to the hotel."

Tex looked over at Mel and smiled. She was really funny. He knew he enjoyed talking to her online, but he had no idea she'd be just as quirky in person.

The rest of the day's drive passed quickly. They went back and forth in sharing more information about themselves and their lives. She'd laughed harder over the last four hours than she had in the last year.

They'd stopped a few times to eat and to let Baby stretch her legs and by the time they pulled up to the hotel that night, Melody felt as if she'd known Tex her entire life. It was dark when they parked in front of the hotel and Melody was exhausted. It was amazing how tiring it could be to sit in a car all day. She noticed Tex rubbing his thigh.

"You want me to go in and get the room?" Melody didn't want to make Tex feel bad, but she wanted to offer.

"No. I'd prefer to take care of it myself. To make sure you're safe here in the truck as I go in and rent us a room, but my leg is killing me and it fucking pisses me off that it'd probably be better if you went in and took care of it for us. I don't think we're in any danger here, as no one has been following us and we're in the middle of nowhere, but I still hate it. You don't mind?"

Ignoring his frustration, Melody calmly told him, "I wouldn't have asked if I did." Melody was surprised Tex actually relented, especially knowing how important it was to him to take care of her and to be in charge.

Tex leaned over and pulled out his wallet and handed her two one hundred dollar bills without a word.

Knowing better than to argue, but planning on paying him back one way or another, Melody took the money. "I'll be right back." Rubbing Baby on her head, she told her, "Be good, girl. I'll be right back." Baby licked her hand then immediately turned and put her head on Tex's leg. Melody smiled, shook her head, and closed the truck door.

She came out five minutes later and opened the truck door. "Head around back. There's a door back there we can use. Our room is on the first floor, on account of Baby."

Tex started the truck and followed her directions. The parking lot was mostly empty when Tex parked. They each got out, Melody holding Baby's leash while Tex carried their bags.

Melody used the swipe card to get them into the building and led the way to their room. She opened the door and Baby pranced into the room as if she didn't have a care in the world.

Melody unclipped Baby's leash and turned to Tex. "I'll take the bags. You go on and get changed. I'll get Baby some water."

Tex put his bag on the floor and handed Mel's bag to her. "I feel like I'm breaking some alpha man code here."

"What do you mean?"

Tex ran a hand through his hair then answered. "I should be the one telling *you* to go and relax. I should be taking care of Baby… I haven't done a good job of taking care of you so far."

"Bull," Melody told him, putting her hand on his arm. "I'm not eighteen years old. I've been taking care of myself and Baby for a while now. And you are doing more for me right now than you'll ever know. You came for me and you found me. I was scared out of my head, I'm still terrified my stalker is going to pop up behind us and attack me. But with you here… I feel like I have a fighting chance. I know you're hurting, and I hate that. So me letting you get changed and get off your feet… well, off your foot… isn't going to mean you have to turn in your man-card. Okay?"

Tex took a faltering step to her and tagged her behind the neck. He drew her to him and put his lips against her forehead. "Thanks."

Putting her hands on Tex's waist, Melody leaned into him and asked, "For what?"

"For being a great traveling companion, for trusting me, for letting me take you home, for knowing I'd kill to lay on that bed and get off this leg."

Not knowing what to say, Melody simply said, "You're welcome."

Tex lifted his head, looked her in the eyes, then leaned down. He kissed her once, hard, running his tongue over her bottom lip, but not giving her time to deepen the kiss. He pulled back. "Go see if you can find an episode of COPS. I'll be right out."

Melody watched Tex as he turned and entered the bathroom. She stood there for another moment, until she heard the water in the sink come on. She shook her head, kicked off her shoes, and walked over to the dresser. She put her bag on top and dug through it until she found a clean T-shirt to sleep in and another pair of boxers. She dug in another small bag and got Baby's bowl out and filled it at the sink with water. She put it on the floor and went back over to the television and turned it on. She stood in front of it flipping through the channels.

When Tex walked out of the bathroom she was still standing there. "I can't find it," Melody told Tex in a mock devastated voice.

"It's okay. I'm not sure we'd be able to stay awake to watch anyway."

"Don't think you're getting out of it. I'm making it my mission in life to introduce you to the best show on TV today."

Tex shook his head at her. "God, you're cute. Go on. Your turn in the bathroom."

"Don't touch that leg. I'll take care of it when I get out."

"Okay."

"I mean it, Tex."

Tex grinned. She read him so easily. "All right. I'll wait."

"Thanks. Get comfortable, I'll be right out."

Tex looked behind him at the king size bed. He hadn't told her what kind of room to get, but she'd chosen a room with only one bed. He didn't want to read into that, but he couldn't help it. He pulled back the covers and climbed in, propping the pillows up behind him. Placing the lotion on the bed next to his hip, he put his head back and closed his eyes. He felt

Baby jump up on the bed. She padded up to him, lay down next to him and nudged his hand.

Without opening his eyes, Tex ran his hand from the top of Baby's head, to her tailbone, then he did it again. Then again. The soothing motion must have relaxed the dog because he felt her practically melt into the bed next to him.

When Melody walked out into the bedroom not too much later, she smiled at the man and dog on the bed. Both were fast asleep and were snoring quietly.

Melody didn't want to wake Tex, but knew he had to get his leg off. She walked over to the other side of the bed, and carefully broke the suction on his prosthetic. It popped off and Melody heard Tex's voice above her head.

"Sorry I fell asleep."

"It's fine. I got this. Close your eyes." She watched as he did just that. Feeling gooey inside that this alpha ex-SEAL was trusting her to do what he needed done, she got back to work. Melody peeled off the liner and reached for the lotion. Melody worked it into his stump, making sure to not put too much pressure on the sore spots, but pressing hard enough on his overused muscles to try to ease some of his aches.

When she finished, she wiped her hands on the sheet, figuring the staff would wash the sheets before the next guests stayed anyway. Before moving away from

Tex, she leaned down and placed a soft kiss right on his stump. She sat up and looked up. Tex's eyes were open and he was staring at her in wonder.

Without another word, Melody walked around the bed and climbed in on the other side. She didn't have the heart to move Baby, so she spooned her dog and faced Tex. He'd turned to watch her progress as she walked around the bed and he was now on his side facing her. They both smoothed their hands over the dog between them, and when their hands nudged each other, Tex grasped Melody's fingers with his own.

As if they were in church, Tex kept his voice low and reverent. "No one has taken care of me like you just did since I was a little kid." He cleared his throat and continued, "I don't know what you see in me, Mel, but it feels good."

"You're a good man, Tex. You're sexy as hell and if we both weren't exhausted I might be tempted to show you just how sexy I think you are."

Tex grinned sleepily at her. "I'll be damned if I try to convince you otherwise."

"Good. 'Cause you wouldn't be able to."

"You always sleep with Baby?"

Allowing him to change the subject, Melody snorted. "Not hardly. She had a nice fluffy dog bed that she used to sleep in at the side of my bed."

"Looks like that's changed."

"Yeah."

They looked down at the dog's side, which was moving up and down under their clasped hands.

"She's a great dog."

"Yeah," Melody repeated.

"I'll look after her too, Mel."

Melody looked over at Tex in surprise. "But—"

"No buts. She means something to you so she means something to me. I'm not going to let him kill her if I can help it."

Tears filled Melody's eyes, and she pulled Tex's hand up to her mouth, kissed the back of it, then brought their hands back to Baby's side. "Thank you," was all she could get out, and her voice hitched anyway.

"As much as I love your dog, she better not get used to sleeping between us. I'm not into doggy voyeurism."

Melody shut her eyes and chuckled. She opened her eyes again and found Tex still watching her intently.

"Get some sleep, Mel. One more long day on the road before we get back to Pennsylvania. We'll have to figure out what's going on and what our next step is. But I'll tell you this, as soon as things calm down, and we have a minute to ourselves where we aren't exhausted or trying to figure out what a crazy person will do next, I plan on showing you how much you're starting to mean to me."

Melody bit her lip and nodded. She couldn't wait.

Chapter Eight

MELODY TURNED OFF the engine to the truck and gripped the steering wheel tightly. She and Tex had talked that morning and decided to push through and go all the way to Pennsylvania. About halfway through the trip, Melody had convinced Tex to let her drive. Once again, he wasn't happy about it, but his leg was hurting more and more and he'd reached a point where it was too painful for him to drive. He'd given her a million instructions and had only shut up when she'd snapped that she wasn't an idiot and had been driving since she was sixteen.

To his credit, he hadn't resisted when Melody had insisted he allow her to drive. After his lecture, and her snarky response, he'd only nodded and when they'd stopped to let Baby take a break, he handed her his keys, kissed her, and headed for the passenger side of the truck.

Melody had tried to push down how nervous she was to be back at her apartment complex. The last time she'd been home she'd been scared out of her mind and Melody wasn't sure she'd ever see it again.

On one hand, she was glad to be back at her place, but on the other, she was scared. She trusted Tex, but was still terrified to be back in her hometown where everything had started.

"Hey, look at me."

Melody jumped when Tex put his hand on her shoulder, and she turned her head toward him. She could just make him out in the dim light of the parking lot.

"It's going to be all right, Mel. I'm going to take care of this for you."

Melody nodded jerkily.

"Stay there, I'm coming around." Tex got out of the truck and went around the front, not breaking eye contact with Melody as he walked around to her side. He opened the door and as Melody stepped out, he crowded her against the side of the truck.

Tex put his hands on the seat behind her and leaned in. He sighed as Mel put her arms around his waist and held on to him. He could feel Baby nudging his arm, but he ignored the dog for the moment.

He rested his chin on Melody's shoulder and turned so he could whisper into her ear. "I know you're scared, but I'm so proud of you for staying strong. You aren't alone anymore. I'm here."

He felt her breath hitch once, before she locked it down again. He buried his nose into the space between her neck and shoulder and wrapped his arms around her, pulling her into his embrace.

They stood there in the parking lot for a few minutes before Tex finally pulled back. He brought his hands up and framed her face. "I mean it." His words were simple and heartfelt.

"I know. I feel like I've dragged you into this, whatever *this* is."

"Mel, you didn't drag me into anything. I brought myself into it. And if I didn't want to be here, I wouldn't be."

Melody licked her lips and finally, after a moment, whispered, "Okay."

Tex leaned toward her and kissed her on the lips. "Now, give me your keys and you and Baby stay here for a moment while I go and check your apartment out. I'll be right back and we can go inside and get some sleep. Tomorrow you can call Amy and we'll start figuring out what's going on. Hop back in and lock the doors and if you see anything that is out of the ordinary, or that scares you, lean on the horn and call me."

"Do you think he knows I'm here? Am I in danger? Are *you* in danger?"

Tex put his forehead against Melody's and put his hands on her waist and squeezed. "Calm, Mel. No, I don't think you're in danger. There's no way in hell I'd leave you sitting out here by yourself if I did. It's just a precaution. I have no idea if he knows you're back in town yet, but I won't be gone longer than a couple of minutes. You haven't been home in months, and I just want to make sure all's well with your place before we go sauntering in there."

Tex didn't mention that he wanted to make sure the stalker hadn't broken in and destroyed everything in her apartment. It was a possibility and he wanted to spare Mel that. He honestly didn't think the stalker knew they were back in town yet, so she should be safe enough while he checked things out. Tex drew back and put his hands on either side of her jaw and looked her in the eyes. "I wouldn't deliberately put you in danger, Mel. Okay?"

Melody sighed and then nodded. She reached into the truck for her purse. Baby, thrilled she could reach Melody's face, licked at her until Melody laughed and pushed her away. "Move, Baby, I gotta get my purse so we can go inside." As if she understood, Baby sat on her haunches and watched as her mistress pawed through her bag and pulled out the key ring she hadn't used in at least half a year. She turned and dropped it into Tex's outstretched hand.

"Be careful." At Tex's raised eyebrows Melody blushed, but refused to look away from him. "I know you were a SEAL and you could probably just look at someone and scare the hell out of them, but we don't know what this person is capable of."

"I will. Promise." Tex didn't waste time reassuring her, he just kissed her on the forehead and said, "Climb back in and shut and lock the door. I'll be back before you know it."

Melody did as Tex requested and watched as he strode confidently across the parking lot and disappeared into the hallway that led to her apartment. Baby whined next to her, and Melody pulled her into her lap, both to comfort the dog and herself. Baby had always been affectionate, but now that they'd been separated for so long, she was even more so. The dog nuzzled into Melody and rested her muzzle on Melody's shoulder. The two sat in the truck and waited for Tex to reappear.

Tex looked around Mel's apartment carefully. It was quiet and dark. It smelled normal, well as normal as a place that had been closed up for several months could be. It was a bit musty and stale. Flipping the light switch next to the front door, Tex tensed as if waiting for someone to pop out of the darkness. All was quiet.

The door opened up into a small hallway which led into a living area. There was a dark brown leather sofa sitting in the middle of the room with a brown and black coffee table in front of it. A large flat screen television was mounted on the wall across from the couch. A brown and black bookshelf sat against another wall. It was filled with books and had pictures scattered amongst the shelves. There was a small dining area that had a table that could seat four people and the kitchen was off to the side.

Tex took a step inside the room and looked into the kitchen. There was a stainless steel refrigerator and dishwasher and a four burner electric stove. The fridge held a few pictures, he assumed were drawn by Amy's kids. The cabinets were maple in color and the counters were granite.

Tex headed to the hallway opposite the kitchen off of the living area. There were four doors, three of which were standing open. Tex opened the door that was shut and saw that it was a linen closet. He moved down the hall and looked into a guest bedroom that held a double size bed and a dresser. The door across the hall from it was a bathroom.

Still vigilant, Tex headed for what had to be Mel's bedroom. He stopped in the doorway and took in her personal space. The bed was a queen size captain's bed. There were drawers underneath and two columns of cabinets and drawers lining each side of the bed. There was a television sitting on a stand opposite the bed. Other than that, the room was empty of other furniture. A large rectangle rug was sitting on the area between the bed and the TV. He looked down and smiled for the first time. Baby's dog bed was sitting next to the bed, just as Melody had claimed.

He turned and peeked into the small bathroom off to the side. It was functional and clean. All looked good in her apartment. For the first time, feeling relieved he hadn't found anything unusual or that would frighten Mel, Tex looked around her room with the eyes of a man, rather than with the eyes of a SEAL.

The room was comfortable and womanly. He could imagine Mel sleeping there. Hell he could imagine both of them sleeping... and loving there. He felt himself grow hard just imagining it. It was almost ridiculous how easy he was aroused just thinking about Melody. One part of his brain told him it was crazy, that he just met her. But the other part argued that it was right, that they knew each other very well after their long online talks.

Before he was injured, Tex was always the one to take the first step in any relationship, whether that relationship was long-term or a one night stand, but with Mel, he didn't want to mess anything up. He'd lost his confidence after being rejected one too many times by women who didn't want to get involved with a crippled veteran. Even his status as an ex-SEAL wasn't enough to entice them.

Tex halted his thoughts in their tracks. Melody was sitting unguarded in the parking lot, probably worried about him. He hadn't lied to her saying he thought she'd be safe while he went inside, but he still needed to stop daydreaming and get her inside where it was safer. He willed his erection to subside as he headed back to the parking lot and the woman who was quickly becoming the most important thing in his life.

Melody sat up straighter in her seat as she saw Tex coming toward her. He didn't look worried, just focused on getting back to her. Baby lifted her head as if she knew Tex was coming, and turned in his direction. Her tail started wagging, but she didn't climb off of Melody's lap.

Tex came over to the driver's side of his truck and opened the door after she unlocked it. He didn't make her wait or ask. "Everything looks fine. Let's get you guys inside."

Melody nodded and clipped Baby's leash on before she stepped out of the truck.

Tex opened the back door and got out their bags. He reached for Melody's free hand and was relieved when she grasped it tightly in hers as they walked to her apartment.

He pushed open the door when they reached it and Baby bounced in. Melody laughed and pulled her back long enough to unclip her leash.

"She's happy to be home," Tex commented unnecessarily.

"Yeah." Melody looked around her apartment and sighed. "Me too."

"Come here." Tex grabbed Melody's hand and shut the door with his foot. He walked them both over to the couch and he sat down and arranged her on his lap.

Melody had tried to be strong, but being back in her apartment, back where she'd been so scared, back where she didn't think she'd ever live again, she finally broke down. She could feel Tex soothing his hand down her back and over her head. After a few minutes she tried to control herself. She lifted tear stained eyes to Tex. "Jeez, Sorry. I swear I never cry. I'm not normally like this."

"Nothing to be sorry for, Mel. I'm surprised it took this long."

"It's just that, I was scared to come back here, and now I'm not as freaked since you're here, but I didn't think I'd ever *get* to come back."

"We'll get your life back."

"I hope so."

"We will."

"Okay, Tex."

"Come on, I'm exhausted. I know you are too. Let's get some sleep. Things'll look better in the morning."

Tex held Melody steady as she stood up and he kept a hand on her back as they walked down the hall to her bedroom. Tex steered Mel into the bathroom.

"Get ready for bed, I'll grab our bags and let Baby

out one last time."

"But your leg—"

Tex put a finger against her lips and cut off her words. "You've taken care of me enough, Mel, let me take care of *you* tonight." When it looked like she was still going to protest he simply said, "Please."

He watched as Mel looked into his eyes for a moment, then gripped his wrist and nodded. She pursed her lips and kissed the finger he had held against her. "Okay, I'll be here waiting for you."

Tex smiled down at her. She was completely transparent. She didn't play games with him. She simply told him she wanted him to stay in her bedroom with her. "I'll be back as soon as I can."

Melody nodded and turned for the bathroom. Tex looked down at her dog. "Come on, Baby, want to go outside once more before calling it a night?" Baby's tongue was hanging out of her mouth and it looked she was grinning up at him. He chuckled as he left the room and headed for the front door.

When he came back into her bedroom about ten minutes later, he saw that Melody had changed the sheets on the bed, the old ones sitting in a lump in the corner of the room. Mel was sound asleep, curled into a tight ball as if protecting herself. Something shifted inside Tex. He'd do anything to keep this woman safe, but it went beyond that. It wasn't just that he wanted to keep her safe. He wanted to end everyday by seeing her in their bed. He wanted to wake up next to her, he wanted to listen to her laugh and talk to Baby in the cute sing-song voice she sometimes used.

Somehow Tex knew Mel was it for him. When he'd made the decision to track her down and drive cross country to find her and bring her home, he'd known. He could've called Wolf and his team to go and get her. He could've just shrugged and decided she'd deleted her online account in that chat room because she was blowing him off. But somehow he'd known. She was special.

Feeling emotional, Tex turned to the bathroom so he could get ready for bed. He came out minutes later and sat on the side of the bed she'd obviously left for him. Tex looked over at Baby, who was snoring at the end of the mattress. Knowing he should probably make the dog get up and get into her dog bed on the floor, he just smiled, shook his head and turned his attention to his leg. He removed his prosthetic and quickly rubbed some lotion into his stump.

He didn't do as good of a job as he knew Mel would've, but suddenly it was vital to him that he hold her in his arms. He propped his prosthetic leg up against the drawers next to the mattress and laid back. He turned to Mel, who was sleeping with her back to him, and he curled into her. He'd never spooned a woman before, but with Mel it felt right. Tex put his right arm around her and snuggled into her.

They were both wearing T-shirts and boxers, but Tex could feel Mel's body heat seep into his body.

"Are you all right?" Mel murmured sleepily.

"Shhhh, everything's fine. Go back to sleep."

"Did you rub your leg down?"

"Yes, sweetheart. I'm good. Sleep. I've got you." Tex whispered the words into her ear and smiled as he felt her snuggle back against him as if settling in for the long haul.

"Mmm-hummm."

Tex smiled and closed his eyes. The trust Mel put in him seemed to magically erase all the doubts he'd had about himself since he'd retired from the Navy. He knew she had no idea what she did for him, but Tex did. Holding her in his arms, knowing even half-asleep she worried about him and cared about him, was a feeling he'd never felt before in his life. He'd do anything to keep her safe. Absolutely anything. Protecting Melody, and Baby, was the only thing he'd be focused on for the foreseeable future. *She* was his future. Tex fell asleep holding Mel in his arms, excited about his future for the first time in a long time.

Chapter Nine

"Y ES, IT'S REALLY me, Amy." Melody reassured her friend for what seemed like the hundredth time.

"Are you back for good?"

"I don't know. I hope so." Melody didn't want to lie to her friend. She knew she wouldn't have been able to get away with prevaricating if she'd been standing in front of her friend. Amy knew her way too well and could take one look at her and know when she was lying or leaving something out. They'd known each other too long to get away with not being honest with one another.

"Are you there alone?"

"No, Tex is here with me."

"Tex, huh?"

Melody could hear the teasing in Amy's voice. "Yeah, Tex." Looking over at Tex, Melody knew their conversation sounded like they were in junior high school, but she could only smile. Tex was sitting on the couch next to her petting Baby while she spoke to Amy.

"And he's sitting right here staring at me wondering what the hell we're talking about." She smiled and looked back down at her dog, sleeping so peacefully between them.

"I like him, Melody. I mean, I wasn't sure when he first called me, but he brought you home, I think I might love him."

"Me too." As soon as the words left her mouth, Melody knew they were true. She looked back up at Tex in a panic, wondering if he'd overheard Amy's words and understood what she'd said in response.

"Everything all right?" Tex whispered the words and leaned toward her, looking concerned.

Melody covered the mouthpiece and quickly told Tex, "Yeah, I'm good."

Tex nodded and leaned back into the couch again and continued watching her and petting Baby.

"We need to talk, woman," Amy said sternly.

"I know, I can't wait to see you, Cindy, and Becky."

"They can't wait to see you either."

"But I don't want to put them in danger, Ames."

Melody heard her friend sigh. "I know. Me either. Will you call me later so we can set up when we can get together? I really need to see you. I've missed you."

"I will. I need to talk to Tex so we can figure out where we're going from here."

"Okay. I'm glad you're back. I have a feeling Tex

will figure this all out."

"I hope so. Okay, Love you, Amy. I'll talk to you later."

"Bye."

"Bye." Melody clicked the phone off and sat back against the couch.

"You guys are really close." Tex's words were matter of fact.

"Yeah. One of the hardest things about leaving was not being able to talk to Amy. Yeah, I missed my parents, but it's not the same as not being able to talk to my best friend."

"You ready to talk this through so we can see if we can't figure it out?"

"No, but yes."

Tex chuckled and gave Baby one last pat on the head and stood up. He held out his hand to Mel. "Come on. Let's sit at the table. I need to use my computer to see what I can find and to write everything down."

Melody grasped Tex's hand and let him lead her to her table. He pulled out the chair at the end of the table and when she was seated, took the chair next to her on the side of the table. He pulled over one of his laptops and fired it up.

"How about we start with how you were able to stay away and how you organized it all. Somehow this guy found you while you were in California, and we have to figure out how."

"Wouldn't it be easier to talk about who I think it might be first?"

"Not really. We'll get to a list of suspects in a bit. First, I just want you to talk. Tell me what you did while you were running. Don't filter what you tell me, let me figure that out."

What Tex said made sense. "Well, I left without really thinking everything through. I didn't have enough money to run indefinitely, but I knew I shouldn't use credit cards because they can be tracked somehow. I went to the bank and pulled a couple thousand dollars out of my account so I'd have the cash. I didn't know how smart my stalker was, but I figured using my cell phone and credit cards could lead someone right to me if they knew computers." She stopped when she saw Tex smirk at her.

"Yeah, like I have to tell *you* that."

"Keep going."

"I rented a car. I figured I'd use it until I decided where I was going and what I was going to do. So I'd been gone for about five days when I called Amy to help me. I knew I'd run out of cash eventually, so I filled out a Power of Attorney for her so she could go to the bank and pull money for me. She'd take out cash and mail it to me. I'd give her the address of a hotel, and then as soon as I got the letter with the cash in it, I'd switch hotels. I bought those throwaway phones that you can get at the store with the pre-set minutes. That way the stalker couldn't track me down that way.

"My job is actually really easy to do from anywhere. I work with a system called CART. It stands for Communication Access Realtime Translation. Basically I listen in to an event via Skype and I type what I'm hearing. My typed words are then broadcast to anyone at the actual venue on an app. They can read the words as they watch. There's a little time lag, but not too much. Since all I need is an Internet connection, that allowed me to keep working, even when I was on the run. I kept paying my rent in the hopes that I'd be able to come home eventually. Amy helped by picking up my mail and paying the bills that came through."

"Sounds like you couldn't have done this without Amy," Tex noted with no inflection in his voice.

"Don't," Melody warned in a low voice.

"Don't what?"

"Amy's not involved in this."

"I didn't say she was."

"Bullshit. I can tell what you're thinking. You're thinking that she knew exactly where I was. She had access to my apartment, but she wouldn't do this to me."

"I thought you weren't going to think about it while

you told me what you did, Mel?" When she seemed ready to lose it, Tex quickly tried to calm her down. "For what it's worth, I don't think she's your stalker."

"You don't? Then why that look on your face?"

"Because as much as it sucks, we have to consider everyone, no matter how much it hurts. But remember, I met her Mel. She kept Baby for you. The stalker said he wanted to hurt Baby. Amy had the perfect opportunity to tell you that she ran away, got hit by a car, got sick... anything. But she didn't."

Melody looked down at Baby who was sleeping next to her chair. "Okay, sorry. I just... she's my best friend. I trust her implicitly."

Tex put his hand over Melody's. "I know you do. I didn't mean to imply she was involved, but that doesn't mean someone else you thought you could trust isn't involved or isn't actually your stalker."

Melody took a deep breath. "Okay, That makes sense. I just... I trust Amy as much as I trust you."

Tex picked up Mel's hand and kissed the palm, never losing eye contact. "Thank you for that. Continue?"

Melody curled her fingers in, as if holding in the kiss Tex had placed on her hand and did as he asked. "So yeah, I'd switch hotels every week or so. I'd rent a car when I needed to change cities, paying with cash, of course, then return the car once I was in a place where I could use public transportation. I would use the Internet in local coffee shops or fast food restaurants."

"Was the note you showed me in California the first one you'd received since you left Pennsylvania?"

Melody looked down at her hands. She'd been clenching them as she spoke. "No. I'd received one when I was in Florida. It said much the same thing as the one you saw."

"So whoever this is, he somehow was able to track you to at least Florida and California. Okay, let's talk about your life here."

"Here?"

"Yeah, here in Pennsylvania. Did you date before you left?"

Melody fidgeted in her seat, then suddenly got up to go into the kitchen. "Can I get you anything? A coffee refill?" She turned around to see if Tex wanted anything and shrieked in surprise when he was standing right in front of her. Jesus, he could move quietly.

Tex hated putting Mel through his questions, but he had to find out as much as he could so they could catch this guy. He put his finger under her chin. "You know I'm not doing this to pry, don't you Mel?"

She immediately dropped her head to his chest and sighed. "Yeah, I know. It's just... it's hard. I don't like to think that anyone I know would do this to me. It's just so horrible and evil... and to think that someone I might have dated, or who I know, who I talked to every day and had no idea he wanted to hurt me and kill my dog and my friends and family, is stalking me? It sucks."

"It does suck. I'm sorry."

"I'm also embarrassed for you to hear about how boring my life was."

"What?"

Melody lifted her head so she could see Tex. "Tex, you were a SEAL. You did exciting things all the time. You *lived* your life. Me? I'm boring as hell. I hung out in this small town. Excitement in my life was heading up to Pittsburgh to go shopping. It's embarrassing."

"Mel, it's not embarrassing. Those exciting things you think I did? They sucked. Every last one of them. I killed people, I hunted people, I rescued people who'd been starved, beaten, or raped... hell sometimes all three. Sometimes we weren't able to save them. We had to recover their bodies. There were times when I would've given anything for a so-called boring life as you call it."

"Tex..."

"So anything you tell me isn't embarrassing. One, it's about you and I want to know everything about you, and two..." His voice dropped and his fingers clenched at her sides. "I like the thought of you living here, safe, without anything like the shit I've seen and experienced touching you. I yearn for you to be able to call going up to the city as exciting again. Help me figure this out so you can get back to that as soon as possible."

"Okay. But I need to be doing something while I talk to you. This is stressing me out."

Tex kissed her on the forehead and looked down at her. "No problem."

"Why do you do that?"

"Do what?"

"Kiss me on the forehead? I like it, but sometimes it makes me feel like I'm eight years old."

"Because if I kiss you like I really wanted to, we wouldn't make it out of your apartment today, or maybe not even tomorrow. And the sooner we can figure out who this asshole is in your life, the sooner I can take you to bed and not have to worry about who might be watching or waiting for us to make a mistake."

"Oh."

"Yeah, oh. I'm controlling myself here, Mel, but trust me when I say there's nothing more I want than to take your mouth, to lift you up on this counter, which is at just the right height, and make you come on my mouth, and my dick, over and over again."

Melody could just stare at Tex for a moment. She could feel herself grow slick at his words. Never before in her life had a guy talked to her like that, but with Tex, she liked it. No, she loved it. She could picture how they'd look, and it turned her on.

Tex leaned forward and kissed her on the forehead

again. "God, if you could see the look on your face. I'm going to go back to the table and write down everything you tell me. You stay here and... do something. After we talk we'll head out and make sure we're seen around town. Then you can call Amy and arrange to meet her somewhere. Then we'll come back here."

"And after that?"

"We'll see, Mel. I refuse to rush you."

"I think I want to be rushed."

"Fuck." The word was low and heartfelt, but Tex let go of Melody and backed away to the table. Tex leaned down and ran his hand over Baby's head before he sat back down. He put his hands on the keyboard and refused to look back up at Mel. He was holding on to his control by his fingernails. Knowing that apparently Mel wanted him as much as he wanted her? Torture. Pure torture.

"I didn't date much, but I had the occasional date here and there. I went to high school in this town, so I know a lot of people. I shop here, I bank here. I dated here."

"Give me the names, Mel."

Melody fiddled with the cup of coffee she held in her hands. Her stomach was churning so she didn't want to drink it. "Lee Davis. He was the last guy I dated. We were together for about three months."

"Why'd you break up?"

"He was kinda a jerk."

"In what way?" Tex's voice was hard.

Melody looked up in surprise. "Just little things. He'd always make me pay when we went out to dinner, saying it was because I made more money than him. He'd flirt with the waitress in front of me. Many times he didn't bother to call me back when I'd leave him a message... just in general he was a jerk."

"Why'd you date him in the first place? I can't imagine you'd put up with that."

Melody smiled at Tex from across the kitchen. His earlier words still flitted through her brain. "I think I was lonely. But you're right, as soon as he started doing those things, and stopped trying to impress me, I dumped him."

"Was he upset about it?"

Melody put the cup on the counter and leaned back against it, putting her weight on her hands. "No. I saw him with Diane the next week."

"Diane?"

"Yeah, she was two years behind me in school. She works at the bank."

"All right, who else?"

"Are we going to do this for every man I've ever dated?"

"If we have to."

"Damn. Okay. Let's see. Adam Grant. We dated for

two months. I wouldn't sleep with him, so he dumped me. Jamie Wilde. We didn't last beyond the first date. I left him at the table, he had the worst manners I'd ever seen. Burping, being crass, he even slapped the waitress on the butt as she walked away from the table. I told him I had to use the restroom and I left."

Melody ignored Tex's chuckle and continued, watching as Tex frantically typed on his keyboard as she talked.

"Chris Myles, M-y-l-e-s. He was my longest relationship. We were together for around seven months. We were practically living together. He'd spend the night at my place or I'd spend the night at his. We were going to move in together, and I knew he was planning on asking me to marry him, but at the last minute I couldn't do it. I broke up with him."

Melody took a deep breath, remembering the fight that had ensued the night she told Chris she thought they should break up.

"Was he mad?"

"Yeah. He was mad." That was the understatement of the year.

"What about you? Were you okay?"

"Yeah. That was why I knew I had to break it off. The thought of not being with him didn't devastate me. The thought of actually living with Chris and being with him day in and day out held no appeal to me. I liked him, but it seemed as if I felt of him more as a friend than anything else. He didn't feel the same way."

"Honestly, do you think it could be him?"

Melody turned toward Tex. His jaw was tight, but he'd kept his voice low and controlled. "I don't know. Before today, I would've said no. But you said I had to suspect everyone, so I suppose, but it'd surprise me. He got married about a year and a half after we broke up. He lives in the area, but he's got three kids and the last time I saw him, he seemed genuinely happy with his wife and his life."

"All right. Anyone else?"

"I don't like this, Tex. Hell, I like you. I don't want to talk about past boyfriends with you. It doesn't feel right."

"I'm not liking it either, Mel. The thought of any-one's hands on you, other than mine, makes me want to do something illegal. But if we can be us, if we can be together, we have to figure out who's stalking you and stop it."

"I know." Mel closed her eyes and kept them closed as she finished reciting the names of the guys she dated. "Terry Neal, Larry Page, Don Ramper… I dated them in college. Robert Pletcher was my high school boy-friend. I don't think I've talked to any of them in years. I can't imagine any of them wanting to stalk me. Hell, they probably don't even remember me."

"They remember you, Mel. I can fucking promise you that. Change of plans. I've got all their names down and into my search program. In a few hours I'll have their driving history, credit reports, arrest record, former addresses, current addresses, jobs, salaries, and everything else that might be relevant."

Mel opened her eyes and looked at Tex. "That doesn't sound legal."

He didn't look up, but continued fiddling with his computer. "It's not, but I didn't think you'd mind if it gives us more information than we have right now."

"I don't... but I don't want you getting in trouble for helping me."

Tex did look up at that. Without breaking eye contact with Mel, he shut his laptop and stood by the table. "As I said, change of plans. I consider myself a reasonable man, but I find after listening to you talk about other men who may or may not have touched you, had you, had what I want so badly I'm about to lose my mind, that I'm not so reasonable after all. I need you, Mel. I want you under me. I want to wipe away the memory of any other man who's ever had what I want desperately. We need to get out of here and in public where I can't bend you over the couch or drag you into your room and make love to you all afternoon."

"Do you want to know why none of the men I've been with have made me want to be with them forever?"

"Mel, you need to stop talking about other men," Tex warned in a low voice. "I'm hanging on by a thread here."

Melody continued as if Tex hadn't interrupted her. "I had to make all the decisions in our relationships. Where we'd go to eat. Whether or not Chris and I would move in together. Who would pay for dinner. It went on and on. It was as if the men I dated knew I was a strong business woman and they figured I'd want to make all the decisions about our dating life. What they didn't realize was that it's tiring. I want someone who can take charge of some things every now and then. I'm not talking about a Dominant/submissive relationship, not that I think that sort of thing is bad, but I'm thinking of things like, deciding where we'd go eat dinner, taking charge with paying for things... I know I'm not saying this very well, but I've never had even one man who I've been interested in, make me quake where I stand and make me wet just by telling me he wants me... until now."

Melody stared at Tex, wondering if she'd been too honest. It was her experience that men liked strong take charge women. Would Tex be turned off by what she'd just said? She watched as Tex took a step toward her. Then another. Then he was in front of her.

Tex reached out and grabbed Mel by the waist and hauled her to him. "I gave you a chance, but you just kept pushing. Now hop up and put your legs around my waist." His words were guttural. Melody didn't hesitate. As soon as her legs curled around him, he turned and headed down the hall toward her bedroom.

Chapter Ten

MELODY DIDN'T SAY a word, just watched the muscle in Tex's jaw tick as he carried her into her bedroom. They had a hundred things they should be doing, but she couldn't think of a single one right at that moment. All she could think of was Tex's body moving under hers as he walked.

Tex walked into the bedroom and shut the door behind him, ignoring Baby's whimpers as she was blocked out of the room.

"I can feel your heat against me, Mel. That's so fucking hot." Tex leaned over and put Mel on the bed on her back then leaned over her. "I wish I could promise that I'll make love to you for hours, but the reality is, I'm about to blow just feeling the hint of your wetness and heat against me. It's been a long time for me, but you aren't just an itch I want to scratch. I hope you know that going into this."

Melody nodded, her mouth too dry to comment.

"This first time is, unfortunately, going to be fast for

me. But I swear, I'll take care of you. I won't leave you wanting. I'm glad you don't mind when a guy makes decisions, because I'm way too used to doing it to back off now. I don't want or need a submissive, but I'm probably going to piss you off sometimes with my take-charge attitude. I'll apologize now, but know that I don't ask you to do things because I'm a dick. I ask you to do things because I think they're in your, or our, best interest. I'm bossy. I'm a former SEAL and I've never wanted a woman in my life more than I want you right this moment."

"God, Tex—"

"Take your shirt off."

Without hesitation, Melody brought her arms to the hem of her shirt and tugged it upward. Tex didn't back off, so she had to wiggle and maneuver herself to get it over her head. When she had it off, she watched as Tex ran his eyes from the top of her head down to her waist and back up, stopping at her bra covered chest.

"I'm not skinny…"

"You're not, and I fucking love it," Tex said without hesitation. He moved one hand and shifted his balance to his other hand. He covered her stomach with his hand and pressed down. "Fuck. Soft and womanly. A perfect balance to my hardness. When I take you, you'll cushion my thrusts with your body. I can pound into you without feeling like I'm hurting you. I'll tell you a secret… when you're on top of me, riding me, there will be nothing sexier than the sight of your tits bouncing up and down each time I hit bottom. And when I'm thrusting into you? Watching your body jiggle and move each time I pound in? Fucking heaven."

"Oh my God, Tex."

Tex's hand moved up and covered one of her breasts and squeezed, just a shade lighter than what would've been painful. "Show me your nipples."

Melody thought she was going to have a heart attack. Her heart was beating wildly and she'd never been more turned on in her life. She brought both hands up to her bra and pulled the cups down until her breasts popped up and over the material. The underwire of the bra pushed her mounds up. Melody looked down and gasped. Her nipples were tight and puckered, as if they were reaching for Tex.

"Tell me to stop now, Mel. If you don't want this. If you don't want what's happening between us, tell me now."

Melody looked up at Tex, expecting to see him looking at her body, but instead he was looking her in the eyes. His pupils were dilated and huge in his eyes. While she watched him, he took his hand off her breast and up to her face. He drew one finger down her cheek and lifted her chin with it. Melody felt him lean down and whisper against her lips. "I need you. I've waited for you my entire life. If we do this, I'm not letting you go."

The words came out without thought, but they felt right. They felt perfect.

"Don't stop."

As soon as the words were out of her mouth, Tex's lips were on hers. He wasn't gentle, but instead he plunged his tongue into her mouth and devoured her. Melody gave as good as she got. Their tongues swirled around each other and plunged in and out of each other's mouths. They both used their teeth to nip and play.

Tex pulled back. "Fuck, Mel." He moved, shifted up and looked down at her breasts. Her nipples were still pulled taut. He leaned down and pulled one of them into his mouth. There were no preliminaries, he didn't tease his way down, he just pulled her nipple into his mouth and sucked, hard.

"Tex. God!" Melody's voice was thin and high pitched. She brought her hand up to the back of his head as he rhythmically sucked against her. Just as she didn't think she could handle anymore, he moved to her other breast. Melody writhed under Tex and lifted her hips in search of something.

Tex released her nipple with a pop. "What do you need, Mel?"

"You. I need you."

Tex stood up abruptly and watched as Mel squirmed

on the bed. She was so beautiful, he couldn't wait another second. He ripped the shirt off his body and quickly undid his pants. He reached into his back pocket and grabbed the condom that had been in his wallet forever, then shoved his pants down his legs and off without a thought about his prosthetic. He was as hard as he'd ever been in his life, and he quickly rolled the condom down his length, praying it hadn't expired.

"Yes, Tex. Help me." Melody was fumbling with the clasp at her back, while her hips were still thrusting up toward him.

Standing naked, but not feeling self-conscious for the first time since he'd had his surgery, Tex undid the button on Mel's pants and helped her remove them. Finally they were both naked.

"Since I know the second I get inside you I'm going to lose control, you're going to have to come at least twice before I get in there. I want this to be as good for you as I know it's going to be for me. Maybe in the future I'll let you choose how you want it, but not now. You said you like when a man takes charge? Well, I'm taking charge. Put your hands over your head and keep them there."

Melody tore her eyes away from Tex's body. He was built, everywhere. She couldn't wait to explore him, but apparently now wasn't the time. She'd never had sex like this before, but if the way her body was reacting was any indication, she'd never forget it and would want more just like it… at least from Tex.

"Spread your legs."

Tex watched as Melody immediately complied. He ran his hands up her inner thighs and groaned when he found the slickness that covered them. "Oh yeah, you're so fucking wet, Mel. For me. All for me."

He heard her voice above him, but he was too focused on his prize to hear what she said. He leaned in and nuzzled the crease where her inner thigh stopped. "You smell like… I have no idea what, but I've never smelled anything like it. It's perfect. You're perfect." He shifted and licked her once from bottom to top. "Oh my God, Mel. I love this. I hope you're comfortable because I'm going to be here for a while."

Melody moaned as Tex gripped her legs and widened them even further. She closed her eyes as he settled in, resting his weight on his elbows next to her hips. His tongue was amazing. He swirled, licked, and sucked every inch of her. Melody hadn't ever really paid that much attention to her sex before. It was just… there. The men she'd slept with hadn't bothered either. They might've fingered her a bit or licked her a few times, but none of them had spent the time worshiping her as Tex was.

She stiffened suddenly as Tex took her clit in his mouth and sucked at the same time he flicked his tongue against her. "Tex! I'm coming!" Instead of lightening up, Tex increased his efforts, thrust a finger inside her and drew out her orgasm as she bucked against his face and hand.

Finally he lifted his head, but didn't let go of her. Melody looked down and saw him licking his lips. She blushed.

"Blushing, Mel? Seriously? Jesus, woman. You just get better and better."

"Aren't you going to—"

"Told you two orgasms, Mel. That was only one."

"Tex…" Melody could hear the whining in her voice.

"Turn over."

"What?"

Tex eased back onto his legs. "Turn. Over."

Looking at him, seeing the lust, but also the deeper emotion, Melody turned over, trusting Tex explicitly. She wasn't sure what to do with her legs, but Tex helped her. He tapped her calves and told her to shift. She shifted upward until her legs were folded under her.

"Put your arms over your head again."

Melody did as Tex asked. She felt way too vulnerable on her knees bent over in front of Tex. Her ass had to look huge like this. Her breathing increased and she lifted her head. "I don't think I like this."

"Shhhhh, Mel." Tex ran both hands down her back,

soothing her. "It's okay. I'm not going to hurt you. Trust me."

Melody nodded and put her head back down, deciding if she could trust him with her life, she could certainly trust him with this.

"You have no idea how beautiful you look like this. Your skin is soft and you're completely open to me." Tex inched closer, spreading Mel's legs further apart in the process. He heard Mel whimper, and hurried to reassure her. "Easy, Mel. Fucking beautiful." He ran his hand over her sex, spreading her wetness over his palm. He then took his hand and smoothed it over her ass, watching as her juices glistened in the light. He did it again, and again. When Mel started shaking, he soothed her once again.

"Easy. I'll get you there."

Tex couldn't believe he was here. Couldn't believe he was here with Melody. He hadn't planned it, but he couldn't imagine his life without her in it now.

Spreading the cheeks of her ass he leaned down and licked her sex. Pulling back, he used his fingers to explore her intimately. Tex pushed a finger inside her and curled it to rub against the sensitive spongy wall inside. Mel jerked and moaned. Tex put a hand in the small of her back and pressed. "Easy, Mel. Hold on for me. Don't let go yet."

"I'm going to…"

"No. Hold it, Mel. Don't come."

He could see Melody hold her breath, then he heard as it came out in a rush. She did it again. Her butt clenched and her toes curled against him. She was doing everything she could to hold off… for him. Tex hadn't ever been so hard in his life. He wanted to plunge inside her more than he wanted his next breath, but he'd been honest with her earlier. He knew the second he pushed inside her tight sheathe, he'd be a goner.

"That's it, Mel… It's going to feel so good when you finally let go. But not yet… hang in there just a little longer."

"Tex, please… your hands feel too good. I need you."

"I can feel you clenching against me. You're gonna be so tight. You want me in there don't you?" His question was rhetorical, because he could feel how much she wanted him.

When her entire body was shaking, Tex said the words she'd been waiting for. "Now, Mel. Come for me *now*."

She did, and it was beautiful. Every muscle in her body tensed and shook. She threw her head back and moaned long and low. Her fingers gripped the pillow-case by her head as she shivered. "Please, Tex, now. Come inside. I want to feel you."

Tex turned Melody until she was on her back again.

He took her ankles in his hands and bent her knees up until she was fully open. He eased forward until his cock nudged her sex. Thank God he'd had the foresight to put the condom on before they started playing. He was so hard he didn't have to worry about guiding himself in. It was as if his dick knew right where it wanted to go.

They both groaned as Tex finally eased himself inside her. He pushed in until he was in as far as he could go. Placing Mel's legs over his shoulders he leaned down and braced himself on his hands.

"I changed my mind about two, Mel. Reach down and touch yourself. I want one more out of you."

Melody hadn't yet recovered from the most intense orgasm she'd ever had, but she followed Tex's command anyway. She took one hand and snaked it between their bodies until she could reach where they were connected. She groaned as Tex pulled his hips back to give her some room. She couldn't help but move her hand lower and circle his length as he pulled out. She tightened her grip as he pushed back in, loving the groan that escaped his mouth.

"Touch yourself, Mel, not me. I'm holding on by a thread here as it is."

"But I like touching you."

"And I like you touching me. But I'm serious, hands off. I want to feel you squeezing my cock when you orgasm again, but I'm not going to be much help here.

Touch yourself. Make yourself come and take me with you."

Since he put it that way... Mel moved her hand and ran her fingertip around her clit. She immediately arched her back. "I'm so sensitive."

"Yeah, you are." Tex looked down at Mel. She was so beautiful, and she was his. He moved his hips rhythmically. In and out. In and out. He watched as her breasts jiggled and he felt remorse for just a moment that he hadn't had time to worship them. Later. He'd spend time with them later.

He sped up his thrusts. He could feel the tingle in his balls, warning him his release was imminent. "Faster, Mel. I'm close. You're too tight and too wet. I can't hold off. Come on. Let me feel you squeeze me." He leaned down to take one quick taste of her nipples before he lost all control. He sucked one into his mouth and took it between his teeth. He pressed down with just enough pressure to be a bit uncomfortable, but not enough to cause her true pain. It was apparently enough.

Tex felt her inner muscles clamp down on his cock as she exploded once again. She bucked up into him as she orgasmed. He groaned and pushed his way in and out of her body, through her muscles that were still flexing and squeezing against him.

"Oh yeah. Fuck, Mel. Yes." Tex thrust one more

time and held himself still as he emptied himself into the condom. He couldn't help but thrust one more time, then two. Finally when he couldn't hold himself up anymore, he collapsed down practically on top of Mel, partially off to her side.

It was many moments before Tex could bring himself to move. He propped himself up on an elbow, careful not to dislodge himself from her. He knew he had to pull out and get rid of the condom, he just didn't want to leave her yet. He brought up a hand and pushed Mel's hair out of her face. It had gotten stuck in the sweat that now covered her brow.

"You all right?"

"No."

Tex's lips quirked up into a smile. "No? Anything I can do to help?"

"Just let me lie here. You've killed me."

"But what a way to go, huh?"

Melody opened one eye and looked right into Tex's face. He was within an inch of hers and he was smiling. "Yeah. What a way to go."

"Is your leg okay?"

The smile on Tex's face faded and he got serious. "You're amazing. Seriously. You just had three orgasms and you did everything I wanted you to, and practically the first words out of your mouth are to ask if *I'm* all right?"

"Yeah. Are you?"

"Yeah, Mel. I'm perfect. You know what? For the first time since that fucking bomb blew up, my leg doesn't hurt. Not even a twinge."

Melody closed her eyes and pulled Tex down to her. "Now I know what to do when it hurts again. It's a new treatment for the phantom pains."

Tex laughed and pulled out of Mel with a groan and pulled off the condom and tied it off.

"The not-so-sexy part of sex," Melody commented wryly. "Just put it on the floor, we'll deal with it in a while."

Tex did as she suggested, then turned back and gathered her into his arms. "Your practicality is one of the things I like about you the most. That and your perfect body."

"Hush. I'm basking."

"Basking?"

"Yes, now shhhh."

Tex just shook his head and shushed. They had things to do. He knew Amy would be chomping at the bit to see her friend, but they had time to relax for a bit longer.

Chapter Eleven

TEX WATCHED AS Amy and Mel cried in each other's arms. After they'd gotten out of bed and cleaned up in the shower, which involved both of them orgasming again, they'd spent some time outside with Baby, then left to try to meet up with Amy. They hadn't gotten two steps away from the apartment when Baby had started howling relentlessly.

Tex looked over at Mel who had an astonished look on her face.

"I take it she's never done that before?"

"No, never."

Tex had calmly opened the apartment door and snapped his fingers. Baby immediately stopped howling and sat on the floor by the couch watching Tex with her tail swishing back and forth on the floor.

"All right, Baby, you can come with us this time."

As if she could understand English, Baby trotted over to the door and waited patiently for Melody to clip on her leash.

They walked out the door again and after Tex re-locked the door headed to Tex's truck. They'd stopped at the bank where Mel had pulled out some cash. She'd spoken for a while to Diane, the woman she knew from high school, as well as another woman who came into the bank while they were there.

When they'd left, Mel had explained the other woman was Heather Wallace. Melody met her in college and while they weren't close friends, Heather seemed very happy to have seen her again.

Mel had used Tex's phone to call Amy and they'd agreed to meet at a fast food restaurant down the street. Now Tex watched as the two best friends were reunited.

"I'm so glad you're okay! I missed you so much!"

"I know, I missed you too, Ames."

Amy reared back out of Melody's arms and smacked her on the arm. "Don't do that shit again."

"He said he was going to hurt you. And Becks. And Cindy. And Baby. And my parents. I couldn't let that happen. I never would've forgiven myself if he hurt you."

"Hashtag best friends."

"Hashtag separated at birth."

Tex watched as the women smiled at each other. He couldn't resist butting in. They were so damn cute together. He'd never thought the things women did with each other as funny before, but now that he'd gotten to know his friends' women better and watching Mel and Amy together, he found that he liked it. "Hashtag you guys are too cute."

"No. You don't get to hashtag," Amy said immediately and seriously, glaring at Tex, not releasing Melody.

"It's ours," Melody tried to explain to Tex gently. "We started it our senior year in high school. It was our 'thing.' Twitter had just started and we were using it and saying it before it was even popular and people knew what it meant. It drove other people crazy, but it was just between us. As typical teenagers we drove our teachers and parents nuts with it. I think there were some days we didn't say anything that didn't start with 'hashtag.' We loved it. Most people hated it."

Amy and Melody looked at each other and smiled, obviously remembering good times.

"Okay ladies. No more hashtagging from me." Tex reassured them. "Come on though, let's get out of the main thoroughfare and you guys can continue your reunion." He steered them out of the middle of the parking lot and away from the prying eyes of anyone who might be in the restaurant or driving by.

He watched as the women talked about Amy's kids and how they were doing. Amy caught Melody up with the local gossip. Amy spent some time loving on Baby, who was very happy to see her. Finally, after thirty minutes or so, they'd gotten most of the basic information out of the way.

Amy kept her arm through Melody's and turned to Tex. "Now what? What can I do to help?"

"No, Amy," Melody told her seriously. "I don't want you involved."

"It's too late, Mels, I'm already involved. This asshole threatened me and my family. He doesn't get to do that and get away with it."

"Amy is right," Tex broke in. "At the very least, I need to talk to her to get her opinion on who might be doing this. She'll have a different viewpoint than you and could really help."

"I'm okay with that, Tex, but I'm not sure about anything else."

"Mel, I told you before, and I'll say it again. I wouldn't do *anything* that would put you or your friends in jeopardy. I honestly think this has to be someone here in your hometown. Face it, it's not like you're a world traveler or anything."

Amy giggled and tried to stifle it when Melody glared at her.

Melody sighed. "Okay, but…"

"No buts."

"God, you can be annoying," Melody huffed out.

"Shut it, Mels. He's not annoying," Amy told her. "He's hashtag cute hashtag protective."

"Hashtag you might be my best friend but I can still

kick your butt."

"Okay ladies," Tex said laughing, "Amy, we'll be in touch. I'm thinking we need to show ourselves around town some more, get whomever it is to see us together and hopefully make him emotional enough to make a mistake."

"Keep her safe." Amy's voice was dead serious and aimed at Tex. "I could handle not seeing her for the last few months simply because I knew she was out there somewhere... alive. I *can't* handle it if she's dead."

"She will *not* get dead." Tex's response was just as serious as Amy's. He endured her intense look and inwardly sighed in relief when she nodded.

Amy turned back to Melody and put her hands on her hips. "Hashtag I think you have a lot to tell me, Mels."

"I love you, Ames. Watch your back." Melody hugged her friend.

"Love you back. You too."

Tex watched as Amy walked over to her car on the other side of the parking lot and got in.

"Come on, Mel, We have a date downtown to go shopping."

"Shopping?"

"Yup, what better place to be seen then downtown, the hub of the town? Since we have Baby we can't go to the mall, we'll do that maybe tomorrow. But for now we'll see who else you know that we can run into. I want this done."

"Me too."

"All right then, let's go. The sooner we get this over with the sooner we can go back to your place."

Tex helped Mel into his truck and walked around and got in. They parked downtown and they all got out. Melody held onto Baby's leash and they wandered around. Tex was amazed at how many people Mel actually knew. It seemed like every time they turned around, someone else was welcoming her home. They'd decided to tell people she had been gone because of work, and since no one really knew much about what a closed caption reporter did, it was easy to be vague in the explanation.

Tex paid close attention to both the people they met and Baby as they walked and talked with people. He tried to catalog people's responses. They met up with several people who seemed genuinely pleased to see Melody, and others who were pretty fake in their response to her.

Baby only growled once, at Lee Davis. Lee was the last guy Mel had dated before the stalker started leaving her notes and threatening her. Tex remembered Mel had told him he'd been a jerk, but he was now dating the girl who worked at the bank... Diane.

Mel hadn't moved to shake his hand or hug him or

anything, but that hadn't stopped him. He'd gone to embrace Melody, but Baby got between them and growled. Lee had quickly stepped back and ended their conversation not much longer after that.

The other person who Baby and Tex didn't like was Robert Pletcher. He'd been Mel's high school boyfriend and Tex hated him on sight. Tex just knew this was the man who'd taken Mel's virginity. He shouldn't have cared, it was a long time ago and he had no right to be pissed about it, or jealous, because he didn't even know Melody back then. But he still felt it. He clenched his teeth when Robert kissed her on the cheek.

Tex couldn't stop his actions, he stepped up to Mel and put his hand on the small of her back. He leaned down and whispered in her ear, loud enough for Robert to hear him. "Baby and I will be right over there." Tex pointed at a bench not too far away. "Take your time visiting with your old friend." Then he put one hand on her cheek and turned her head to face him. He swooped down and kissed her. Not quick, and not softly. Pulling back he brushed his knuckles over her cheek and grabbed Baby's leash and headed for the bench.

When he got there he sat down, crossed his arms, and watched as Mel spoke with Robert. Baby jumped up on the bench next to him and sat as if she was human. Tex put his hand on her back and stroked while they waited for Mel.

Within five minutes she finished her conversation with Robert and walked toward them, smiling. She sat down next to Tex and put her hand on his thigh. She leaned over and patted Baby on the head and sat back.

"You wanna explain that?" Melody asked Tex.

"Do you *need* me to explain it?"

She smiled. "I don't think so. Tex, you have nothing to be worried about where Robert's concerned."

"It's not that I'm concerned, Mel. I don't think you're suddenly going to dump me and declare your everlasting love for that schmuck. I just don't like knowing that you and he…"

Melody stretched up and kissed Tex quiet. "It was forever ago. And it wasn't even good."

"Doesn't matter. We could be eighty years old and I still wouldn't like it."

Melody giggled. "Come on. Can we go home now? I didn't get to explore earlier." Just as the words were out of her mouth Tex was up and walking quickly toward his truck, Mel's hand held tightly in his own.

"We'll stop and pick up dinner on the way back to your place." Looking down at Baby as they walked Tex apologized. "Sorry, Baby, you're going to be on your own again tonight. Gotta spend some quality time with my girl."

Chapter Twelve

MELODY STRETCHED AND winced. She was sore in places she'd never been sore before. Well, at least without spending hours in the gym. Tex had been amazing last night. He'd let her play to her heart's content, then spent just as much time returning the favor.

She turned over only to find an empty bed next to her. The sheets were cold, but Melody could see the imprint of Tex's head in the pillow next to her. Looking at the clock, Melody saw it was seven in the morning. She was usually up before now, but Tex had tired her out last night. She stumbled into the bathroom, grabbing her T-shirt and boxers off the floor where Tex had thrown them last night.

After her morning routine, she padded out into her living room and stopped dead. Tex was there. He was currently doing pushups and Baby was keeping him company. She was trying to lick his face every time he pushed himself up. Melody had no idea how long Tex had been at it, but since he hadn't noticed her yet, she leaned against the doorjamb to watch.

Even though Baby looked like she was being annoying, Tex tolerated her interference in his workout regime with extreme patience. It was amazing to see him doing one legged pushups. Oh, he was using his prosthetic to balance himself, but Melody could see that all of his weight was on his good foot.

Tex turned over after a few more pushups and started doing sit-ups. Baby obviously thought this was a fun new game, because she stood over him and tried to climb into his lap every time he laid back on the ground. Finally he gave up and mock growled and grabbed Baby around her body and fell backward with the dog in his arms. Baby wiggled out of his grasp, but came right back at him.

Melody watched as man and dog roughhoused on the floor. Both looked like they were having the time of their lives. Melody realized she hadn't been this happy in a long time. She'd spent the last six months being scared and worried and she always woke up tense, wondering what the day would bring.

Tex had brought her some peace. She knew she wasn't out of the woods yet, but whatever happened, Tex would be there to help her figure it out. She didn't want to think about what would happen if her stalker didn't make a move. Or once he was hopefully caught.

She lived here in Pennsylvania and Tex lived in Virginia. He was staying with her right now, but that wouldn't be forever.

Melody shook her head, refusing to think about the future. She'd just thought about how happy she was, she didn't want to ruin it.

Baby must have seen her movement because she struggled out of Tex's hold and leaped over to Melody.

She laughed, kneeled on the ground and greeted her. Baby really was a good dog. Even though she'd been locked out of the bedroom last night, she didn't hold any grudges toward her or Tex.

"Good morning, beautiful," Tex said above her. He'd gotten up and walked over to where she and Baby were.

"Help me up." Melody held out her hand to Tex. He immediately grabbed it and lifted her off the ground as if she weighed nothing. He didn't just help her up, but pulled her right into his arms.

"Good morning, beautiful," he repeated.

"Good morning, Tex." Melody blushed at the intense look Tex was giving her.

"I have no idea how you can blush after what we did last night, but I love that you do."

"Did you sleep okay?"

"Mel, I've never slept better in my entire life, and certainly not since my surgery. Holding you in my arms, listening to you breathe, knowing you were exhausted from the orgasms I'd given you… fucking perfect." Tex leaned down and kissed Mel long and hard. He pulled back and watched as Mel chewed on the corner of her bottom lip. "What is it? What aren't you saying? Come on, Mel, don't hold back."

"You weren't there this morning when I got up."

"You have nothing to worry about, swear to God. Mel, I was a SEAL. I'm used to getting by on a lot less hours sleep than you. I work out every morning. Even though I'm retired, I haven't broken the habit. As it was, I laid in bed for twenty minutes just listening to you breathe and feeling you against me. I probably would've stayed there if I didn't hear Baby outside the door."

"It's just…" Mel paused, knowing what she was going to say would sound needy, and not really wanting to seem that way to Tex, especially since they hadn't been together very long.

"Come here." Tex took Mel's hand and led her to the couch. As was his usual, he sat down and pulled her into his lap. "Now, go on, tell me what's going on in that brain of yours. I know this is new, but you weren't afraid to tell me what you were thinking when we were talking to each over the computer, don't be afraid now that we're face-to-face."

"Will you wake me up when you leave in the morning?" At the frown on Tex's face, Melody hurried to complete her thought. "It's just that... I want to start my morning with you. And I can't do that if you're not there. Oh, I get that you have things to do, you aren't tied to my bed, but if I can't wake up with you, I'd like to know when you get up." Mel took a deep breath and continued, not looking Tex in the eyes. "It's happened before. One of the guys I dated in college left in the middle of the night and never came back. I guess he wanted to break up with me and didn't know how to tell me. I'm a little sensitive about it now."

"What a fucker. Mel, I'm not going anywhere. You heard me when I said you were mine didn't you? That if you wanted me, I was yours? I wasn't kidding. Besides, you need your sleep. I don't want to wake you up."

"I'm not talking about you shaking me and making me get up and do twenty pushups before you go and save the world, run a marathon or whatever." Melody smiled at Tex. "But just kiss me or something. I can sleep anywhere, I won't have any problem falling back asleep. It'll make me feel better knowing you haven't packed up to get out of here and that I could say good morning when you got up."

"All right," Tex agreed immediately, understanding her angst about waking up to an empty bed. "But believe me when I say I'm not fucking going anywhere. We need to have a conversation about what comes next, but until things have been resolved here, I'm not sure we're ready to have it. But rest assured, I'm not going anywhere."

Melody smiled at Tex. "Okay."

"Okay. Now, I don't think I've said a proper good morning yet. Kiss me, Mel. Like you mean it."

"I always mean it," Melody said the words with a smile as she leaned into Tex. She licked a path up the side of his neck. "Mmmmmm, salty."

"Mel…" Tex warned, feeling himself growing hard under her.

"Can't help it. You're just so sexy and masculine, and you're here with *me*. It's all so unbelievable."

Tex didn't answer, just took her head in one of his hands and brought her face to his. He kissed her long and hard. If he had to kiss her to make her believe it, he would… gladly.

When Melody came back to herself, she was on her back on the couch with Tex on top of her. One hand was under her shirt at her braless breast, and the other was holding her knee up, so his erection was notched between her legs in just the right spot.

"Good morning, Mel," Tex whispered huskily, while rubbing the back of her knee with his thumb on his left hand and her nipple with the fingers on his right.

"Did you get your workout done?" Melody asked breathlessly, arching her back slightly, pushing her breast further into his hand.

"No, but I can think of another way to burn some calories."

Thirty minutes later Melody lay on top of Tex on the couch. Clothes had been thrown every which way and they were both mostly naked. Tex had stripped her of her clothes and had made her do all the work since he claimed he'd already worked out. Melody had never been with a lover who was as vocal as Tex was. He'd complimented her throughout their lovemaking, commenting on her body, the way it moved, the way it felt, the way it made *him* feel. Nothing seemed to embarrass him or turn him off. At one point, Melody had reached behind her to try to cup Tex's balls and her fingers had slipped and she'd accidently prodded him in the backside. Instead of tensing up, Tex had moaned and gripped her hips harder and exclaimed, "Oh yeah, Mel, that feels amazing." Of course *she* had blushed and immediately moved her fingers to her intended target, but Tex had just smiled under her and winked.

As much as Melody wanted to go back to bed, she knew they had things to do today. Tex had to check his programs and see what information he could glean from them about the men she'd dated in the past and she had a job today. There was an assembly she had to translate for and she had to read the materials the company had sent for her to review beforehand. She'd taken too many days off driving cross-country and needed to get back in the swing of things.

Feeling Tex's hard body underneath her move slightly, Melody turned her head. He was laughing. "What's funny?"

Tex didn't answer out loud, but instead used his chin to gesture off to the left. Melody turned her head to see Baby sitting nearby. Her head was cocked and her tail was swishing back and forth along the floor. Melody dropped her forehead on Tex's chest and groaned. "Oh my God, we've corrupted my dog."

"So much for doggy voyeurism being out." Tex only laughed harder when Mel groaned against his chest again. "Come on, Mel, shower, by yourself, or we'll never get anything done. Breakfast first and we'll take a look at the results of my searches. Then we'll head out. We need to hit a grocery store and see if we can be seen around town some more."

Melody raised her head and propped herself up on Tex's chest. She looked at him for a moment before saying softly, "Thank you."

"Don't thank me," Tex scolded immediately. "There's nowhere I'd rather be than here with you. I don't care if you had three stalkers, an escaped murderer was at your door, and Baby was rabid and attacking. This is what I've waited my whole life for." When Mel's eyes teared up, Tex sat up, holding tight to her so she didn't fall. He kissed her eyes, one at a time. "Don't cry,

Mel. This is the start of our beautiful life together."

Tex urged Mel to stand up, and when she did, he turned sideways on the couch and buried his head in her stomach, holding her to him. He felt her hands in his hair and on his head. He inhaled deeply, then tilted his head back to look up at her. "You smell amazing." Tex's hands gripped her backside and kneaded. "You smell like us."

"Tex."

Tex took one hand and cupped her sex, then brought that hand up and smeared her wetness on her belly. Without taking his eyes from hers he said seriously, "A beautiful life, Mel. I'm going to do whatever it takes to give that to you... to us. Now, as much as I want to spend all day naked with you, we've got things to do."

Tex caressed her belly one more time, then turned her and smacked her lightly on the ass. "Go shower, woman."

Melody giggled and took a step toward the hallway and her bedroom. She looked behind her at Tex still sitting on her couch. Baby had walked up to him and he had one hand on her head and the other was on his knee. His eyes were glued to her though. Melody put a bit of a sway in her step as she continued toward the shower. She heard him groan behind her and she smiled. Somehow Tex had made coming home fun...

when it should've been nothing but terrifying.

Melody knew some people would claim they were moving way too fast. That having Tex basically living with her was crazy, that she only knew him for around a week, but she knew that wasn't true. She'd known Tex for over six months. Yes, she'd just met him in person, but the groundwork of friendship had been laid for months now. They'd danced around the sexual tension they felt while they were talking online, but had never done anything about it.

She had no idea where they were going or what her crazy stalker would do now that she was home, but Melody hoped like hell in the end, when the dust was all settled, she could find a future with Tex.

Chapter Thirteen

M ELODY SAT AT her kitchen table with her head in her hands as Tex continued to type as he spoke with her.

"Nothing really stands out on the guys whose names you gave me. Your high school boyfriend, Robert, is married like you said he was, but it also looks like he's had a couple of affairs as well, so he's not as devoted to his family as he might make it appear. All of the men you told me about have debt, but Lee is in to it to his eyeballs. It's a good thing you ditched him when you did, Mel. He has three credit cards that are maxed out and it looks like he has a couple of speeding tickets that haven't been paid yet either. Not only that, but the cops have been called to his house at least twice for domestic violence issues."

"Bastard," Melody said with feeling. "Poor Diane. I know I've been gone, and I don't really know her that well, but no one should have to live with that crap. I hope she dumps his ass."

"Yeah, it looks like she's been hospitalized twice in the past at Saint Albin's hospital."

"Saint Albin's?"

"Yeah."

"That's a mental hospital."

"Yup."

"Is she okay?"

Tex sighed. "I can find out exactly why she was there and what her diagnosis was if I dig, but it looks like she was hospitalized before she started dating Lee."

"Well, he can't be good for her, that's for sure," Melody sympathized.

"Can I send this stuff to Wolf and his team to look over?"

Melody looked at Tex in surprise. "You're asking me?"

"Yeah. While I'm good, sometimes it helps to have another set of eyes. And I'm a bit too close to this whole situation to be completely unbiased. So I'd like to get your permission to show this stuff to my friends."

"Then, yeah, you can show it to them. I'm not sure what good it'll do, but it can't hurt."

"Thanks, Mel. You're right. It can't hurt." Tex immediately began tapping out a message on his keyboard. "I'll encrypt it before I send it so it can't be traced back to me, and so the information stays secure. Once I'm done here we need to go to the police station. We should've done it before now, but I got distracted…"

Tex looked up at Melody with a look so hot, she thought she'd melt in her seat.

Tex continued his thought, "I'm assuming you went to them before you headed out on the road?"

"Yeah, there wasn't anything they could do. They took the notes I'd received and made a report, but otherwise they told me just to be careful."

"That's what I thought. Well, we'll bring them the note you got in California, just to get it logged, and to let them know you're back in town. They might not be able to do much, but if anything *does* happen, at least they'll have a head's up."

Melody shuddered at the thought of her stalker catching up with her. "Do you think he's going to do something? I think I'd rather he just did it and got it over with rather than having this drag on and on."

Tex stopped typing and turned to Mel. "I don't know. My gut says he's not going to be happy I'm here with you. I'm guessing it's going to escalate things, and probably quickly. But I could be wrong. It could be he'll just hunker down and try to wait me out. But if that happens, we're good Mel, because I'm not going anywhere. He'll have a hell of a long 'hunker' if that's his plan."

Melody couldn't say anything. The intense look in Tex's eyes floored her, and made her yearn to reach for all the promises she could see in his eyes. Eventually, he looked down at his laptop and broke the sexual tension between them.

"Okay, I've sent the email. Let me get the note and we'll get out of here. If Baby will let us, we'll leave her here today and head to the police station first. Then we'll go to the mall and walk around. If there's any other places you usually hung out at before you left town, we'll stop there too. We'll call to meet up with Amy again today as well, if you want. I know you want to see her kids, but it's probably best at this point to leave that for later. But Mel, I know how much Amy means to you, if you want to see Becky and Cindy, I'll figure it out."

"I'd love to see Amy again today, but yeah, it's probably best if we left the kids out of it for now." Switching the topic, because it hurt to think of Amy's kids and not being able to see them, Melody said, "Let me talk to Baby. I'll see if I can't get her to agree to stay here for the day."

Before Melody moved to have a heart to heart with her dog, Tex pulled her across the short expanse separating them with a hand on the back of her neck. "You're so fucking cute. Tell Baby that if she stays here, I'll bring her home a nice juicy bone." Then he kissed her roughly, nipping her bottom lip as he pulled away.

Melody smiled at Tex, and put her hand on his

cheek briefly. She got up and went over to sit on the couch with Baby. The dog jumped up next to her mistress and immediately demanded pets. "Okay, Baby, here's the deal. I need you to stay home today." Baby started whining before Melody could finish. She knew it was weird that she was talking to her dog as if she could understand her, but Melody figured that deep down, maybe Baby could recognize the emotions and feelings behind what she was saying. So while she wouldn't understand the words, per se, she could tell that something important was being said.

"I know, I know, I've missed you too, but we've been together for like six days straight now. I have to do some things today and you can't go with us. I don't want to have to leave you in the car. It's not safe or healthy for you. So if you stay here today, and be good, Tex said he'll bring you back a nice juicy surprise. You'd like that wouldn't you?" Baby tilted her head up and licked Melody's face and she giggled.

"Okay, Tex, we're all set." Melody said the words semi-loudly, turning her head only to screech in surprise when she saw Tex resting his elbows on the back of the couch right next to her.

"Jesus, Tex, stop sneaking up on me like that!"

"I wasn't sneaking, Mel. I was right there. Baby knew I was here, you were just concentrating too hard on her to notice me."

"No, Tex, even with that fake leg, you walk like a Native American in the forest hunting rabbits. You're completely silent and it's almost eerie."

"Habit, Mel. Habit."

Melody sighed. "I know, you can take the man out of the SEALs, but you can't take the SEAL out of the man."

"Hey, I like that!" Tex told her standing up and running his hand over Mel's hair. "Come on, let's get going."

Melody kissed the top of Baby's head and gave her one last pat. "I'm ready." She grabbed her purse off the counter as they headed out of the apartment.

Baby whined once as they were about to leave, but Tex merely turned around and said sharply, "Baby, stay."

The dog huffed once, then turned and trotted to the couch and climbed on. She settled onto the cushions, resting her head on the back of the couch so she could see them leave.

"She's good at the guilt trip thing," Melody commented unnecessarily.

Tex just chuckled and put his hand at the small of Melody's back to lead her out of the apartment. He locked the door behind them and thankfully Baby was silent as they headed to the parking lot.

Melody looked up at Tex and said, as they walked to

his truck, "How do you get her to obey you so well? She's a hound, she doesn't obey anyone."

He didn't answer and Mel looked at him in confusion. His face had gotten hard and he moved his hand from her back, to grip her elbow. "Looks like the cops will come to us today, Mel."

"Huh?" Melody turned to look in the direction Tex was facing and gasped. His truck had been vandalized. All four tires were flat and both headlights had been smashed and broken. "Oh Tex, your truck."

"It's only a machine. It can be fixed."

As they walked closer to the truck, Melody could see the words that had been spray-painted on the truck. She ignored Tex as he called the police to report it and concentrated instead on the ugly words, the hate, sprayed on Tex's truck.

Bitch. Whore. You'll pay.

Melody realized that Tex hadn't taken his hand off of her elbow and she curled her arm through his and pressed up against his side. She looked around, as if expecting someone to spring from the bushes and attack them.

Tex put his arm around her, but after he hung up with the cops, turned his cell phone around and started clicking pictures of his truck and the area around it. Without looking at her, Tex tried to reassure Mel. "This is actually a good thing. I know it doesn't seem like it, but it is. It means that after only a day, we've gotten to him. He's emotional and pissed. He's seen me with you and he can't stand it. The more emotional he gets, the more mistakes he'll make."

"But your truck."

With her words, Tex lowered his phone and turned Mel in his arms so she was plastered against him. "It's only a truck. I couldn't give a flying fuck about it. Honestly. I'll rent a car today so we'll have transportation."

"We can use my car. It's parked over at Amy's."

"No, I'll rent something. Call it a man thing, or a SEAL thing, or even a boyfriend thing, but I'd prefer to stick close to you until this is done. Let me drive you around, Mel."

"Fine. It doesn't make sense for you to spend money on a car when I have a perfectly good one at our disposal, but whatever."

Tex continued as if they didn't have a side conversation about renting a stupid car. "I'm pissed at myself though. I should've already set up security cameras around your apartment. If I had, I'd have more to go on, but if he's done this now, already, he'll do it again. I'm going to catch him, Mel. I swear to God."

"I'm scared."

"I know, and I hate that. But, Mel, look at me." Tex

tipped Mel's face up so she had no choice but to look at him. "I've just found you after all these months. I'm not going to let anything happen to you. Whoever is doing this is emotional and uncontrolled. That's much better than methodical and calculated. He'll make a mistake and this'll be over. Trust me."

"I do. You know I do. But I still hate this."

"I know. I'm not that fond of it myself. But we'll deal with it… together." They both looked up when they heard sirens coming their way. "I'm going to send the pictures to Wolf, we'll deal with the cops, I'll call a tow truck, then we'll do what we were going to do today before this."

Melody nodded. She tried to control the shaking of her body, and snuggled into Tex as he held her tighter to him. She could do this. She'd been dealing with it alone, just because she had Tex here now to help her didn't mean she wasn't the strong woman that had been on her own for months. She had to suck it up and really analyze everyone around her. She had to help Tex figure this out, not sit back like a pathetic woman who needed protecting.

MELODY SAT ON a bench in the city park with Amy. She'd called and Amy had agreed to meet them there. Cindy and Becky were still in school and her husband was at work. Amy left work early and came straight to the park after hanging up with Melody.

Tex had stayed with Melody until Amy had arrived. Then he'd kissed her on the forehead and said, "Visit as long as you want. I'll be over there." He'd pointed to a bench about a hundred feet away and left her alone with Amy.

"How are you holding up?" Amy asked Melody, holding on to her hand tightly.

"I'm okay."

"Hashtag seriously? Mels, this is me. I know you better than that."

Melody sighed. She loved Amy, but sometimes hated that she couldn't lie worth a darn with her. "I'm scared out of my mind. Tex tells me not to worry, but I can't help it."

Amy looked down at their clenched hands and bit her lip. Then she looked up at Melody and squeezed her hand. "I love you like the sister I never had, Mels. And I know you enough to know what I'm going to say is most likely going to piss you off, but I'm saying it for your own good."

"Fuck," Melody said under her breath.

"How much do you really know about Tex? I mean, you started talking to him online and now he's living in your house and if I read you right, you're sleeping with him. I had him checked out with my connections at work, but what if *he's* your stalker? What if he's the one doing this to you? He found you in California right after you received that note. It looks bad and I wouldn't be a good friend if I didn't bring it up."

Melody stiffened on the seat and wanted to wrench her hands away from her best friend and storm away from her. But she knew Amy loved her and was looking out for her as best she could. Hell, if their roles were reversed, she knew she'd probably think the same thing. Tex had even thought *Amy* could be the stalker. It was an interesting coincidence that Amy also suspected Tex.

Melody looked up at Tex who was sitting across the way and saw he hadn't taken his eyes off of them. He was staring intently at her, always conscious about what she was feeling. She took a deep breath.

"It's not him, Ames." When Amy opened her mouth to interrupt, Melody continued quickly. "Please, let me explain how I know. Okay?" Waiting for Amy to nod, Melody squeezed her hand when she did.

"I was in some hellhole in Mississippi the first time Tex messaged me online. I'd been on the run for a few weeks and was tired and scared. The stalker had already found me in Florida and I was running. Tex messaged me and said he liked my username. He didn't say anything sexual, and he made me laugh for the first time since I'd received the first note. He didn't put any pressure on me, didn't make me feel as if he wanted anything from me. I wasn't going to talk to him again, but when he messaged me again, I couldn't help but respond. He was just as funny, and non-threatening. Amy, I chatted online with him for months, and not *once* did he overstep any bounds. He never asked me where I was, he never asked me for my picture, he never tried to sext me. Six months, Amy. *Six.* How many guys do you know that would do that?"

When Amy stayed silent, Melody continued, "Exactly. He talked to me about his life. He told me about his fears. He told me about how he felt about losing part of his leg. Not one guy I've met in my entire life has opened up to me like that before."

"That doesn't mean he didn't do it to gain your trust, Mels."

Melody knew Amy was just trying to play devil's advocate, but she was getting frustrated with her. She'd have to prove it to her. "He's not like that, Amy. He wants to protect me. He shields me from anything that might be painful. This morning when he saw his truck, the first thing he did was put his arm around me and pull me to his side. His eyes shifted back and forth to search out any threat that might be lingering. He doesn't want to hurt me, Ames. He's the best thing that's ever happened to me. Watch."

Without warning Amy about what she was going to do, she leaned over and grabbed her calf and yelled,

"Ow!" Before Amy could move and before Melody could even look up, Tex was there.

"What's wrong, Mel? Move your hands, let me see." Tex was there, he had her calf in his hand and was massaging it. "Did it cramp up on you? Damn, we did too much today didn't we? We should get you home."

Melody put her hand on top of Tex's head. "I'm okay, Tex. Really. Just a little cramp. It feels better. I'm not ready to go yet."

Tex looked up at Melody, then looked over at Amy. Putting his hand on Mel's face he said seriously, "I don't want you upset. You've got enough going on, if you need to put off whatever conversation you've been having that's made you uncomfortable, you need to do that."

Amy smiled and cut into their talk and laid it out for him. "It's okay, Tex. I told Mels that maybe you were her stalker. She didn't like that."

Melody turned to look at her friend. She didn't think Amy would've come right out and told Tex she thought he was a suspect.

Not removing his hand from Melody's face, Tex turned to Amy. "I insinuated the same thing about you. She didn't take that any better than I bet she took you suggesting that I might be. Amy, I'm not her stalker. I give you my word as a Navy SEAL and as the man who cares about your friend a great deal."

"Good enough for me," Amy said immediately.

"Give us another twenty minutes or so?" Melody asked Tex softly.

"Of course." Tex stood up and kissed Mel on the forehead, which made her smile, remembering what he'd said about why he kissed her there and not on the lips. He did it all the time and she loved it.

As Tex walked back to the bench he'd been sitting on before Melody had faked a leg cramp, Amy commented in a breathless voice, "Hashtag holy shit."

"Hastag told you."

"Yes you did. Now, serious stuff... how is he in bed?"

"Amy!"

"Mels! Spill it!"

Melody squirmed in her seat, but admitted softly. "Amazing. Seriously Ames, I've never experienced anything like it before in my life."

"Does his leg make it weird?"

"His leg?"

Amy looked at her friend as if she were dense. "Yeah, Mels, his leg. You know, he's missing half of it? Is it weird? Does it look gross?"

Melody got mad at her friend for the first time in a long time. "Amy, what the hell? Seriously? His leg is fucking beautiful. You know why? Because it's a part of him. Because losing that leg means he's still here to be with me today. And the answer is no, it's not weird. He made me come twice last night before he even thought about satisfying himself. You think in the middle of that I could even spare a thought about what his fucking leg looks like or that I'd even *care*?"

"Uh, Mels—"

"And besides, his leg is fucking sexy as hell. You wouldn't think it was, but I've already had a fantasy or two about rubbing up against it as I make myself come. And trust me, Tex is the *least* disabled man I've ever met in my life. He might have a bionic leg, but Ames, his mouth, his fingers, and his cock more than make up for *any* disability you or anyone else thinks he might have."

"Mels, seriously—"

"No. That's what's wrong with this world today. People see someone with a limp or a prosthetic and they think something's wrong with them. There's not one fucking thing wrong with him. Not to mention he's a hero. He was a fucking SEAL, Ames. You think missing half his leg would ever slow him down? Hell, given half a chance he'd probably take his prosthetic off and beat the hell out of my stalker with it."

Melody was breathing hard, full of emotion and pissed off at her friend. She didn't mind talking about how great the sex was with Tex, but she'd be damned if she let anyone, including her best friend in the world, talk smack about him.

"Hashtag he's standing right behind you," Amy whispered, smiling at Melody.

Melody whipped her head around and saw Tex standing stock still about four feet from the bench she and Amy were sitting on. He was watching her with an intense look in his eyes. Melody had no idea what to say. She hadn't told her friend anything she didn't mean, but it was embarrassing none-the-less.

"Amy," Tex started without taking his eyes off of Melody. "Your friend is the best thing that has ever happened to me. I know most women feel the way you do about my prosthetic, but I've never had anyone stand up for me the way Mel just did. So while I don't mind if you want to girl-talk about our sex life, I don't like seeing Mel upset." He finally turned to look at Amy. "So if you want to know about my leg, in the future please ask *me*. You want to see it? I won't like it, but we can have a show and tell anytime you want. But I'd appreciate if you keep your thoughts about how weird it might be to have sex with me to yourself, simply because it upsets Mel."

"I didn't mean anything by it, Tex. I'm sorry," Amy told him in a small voice.

Tex nodded and turned back to Mel. "You about ready to go?"

"Can you give me a second?" Melody didn't think he was going to do it, but finally he nodded and stepped back about ten feet and turned his back to the bench. Melody figured he could probably still hear them, but she didn't want to push it.

"Mels, I'm sorry, I didn't mean..."

"No, I know you didn't, I overreacted," Melody tried to tell her friend.

"No, you didn't. You defended him and rightly so. I was being a bigot and stereotyping him. If George had a disability like that and you said something rude to me as I did to you, I would've done the same thing." Amy dropped her voice to a whisper, "I love my husband, and it's obvious you love Tex. I'm thrilled to death for you that you have someone you feel that passionately about. Now, go back to your apartment and have some wild and crazy sex. The next time we meet up you can tell me all about it, hashtag without me being a bitch about his leg."

"I love you, Ames."

"I love you too, Mels. Now go. I have a feeling Tex is gonna catch this asshole sooner rather than later and you'll have your whole life to look forward to."

Melody smiled at Amy and hugged her once they stood up.

Tex came over as Amy was walking away and took Mel's hand in his own. "Ready to head home?"

"Yeah, about what I said..."

"Just so you know, I have a feeling Baby isn't going

to get to sleep in our bed anytime soon. We don't want to corrupt her beyond all repair."

Melody smiled and teased Tex back as they walked to the rental car. "Yeah? You haven't changed your mind about the doggy voyeurism huh?"

Tex hooked one arm around Melody's neck and put another hand at her back and dipped her backward, ignoring her girly screech. "Frankly, as soon as I get a whiff of your arousal I forget everything else. Baby, where we are, the damn stalker... all I think about is tasting you, seeing you orgasm, and getting inside you. I'd apologize, but I know as soon as my lips hit yours, you're just as lost as I am."

"Tex. Jesus. Stop. Seriously. Let me up."

Tex leaned down and nuzzled her ear, still holding her practically upside down. "Are you wet for me, Mel?"

"You know I am."

Tex brought Mel upright and shook his head. "No games. I love it. Come on, let's get home. I have plans for you."

Mel gladly took Tex's hand and followed along beside and behind him. All thoughts of the stalker, someone that might be watching or following them, were gone from her head. All she could think about was what Tex might do to her, and what she wanted to do to him. She couldn't wait.

Chapter Fourteen

"I HATE THIS!" Melody complained, holding her head in her hands at her table. Baby whined next to her, sensing her mistress' distress. Melody felt as if she was suffocating. The last two weeks had been idyllic in one sense. She loved having Tex living with her. He was an easy person to share a space with. He wasn't perfect, but the things he did that were a little annoying, were way overshadowed by the many ways he helped make life easier around the apartment. He cleaned up after himself, he didn't leave little black hairs in the bathroom sink after he shaved, he cooked, he cleaned, hell, he even walked Baby when Melody couldn't bring herself to get out of bed.

It wasn't him. It was everything else. She didn't have a minute to herself. If Tex wasn't with her, he left her with Amy with strict instructions not to move until he came back to get her. He'd made good on his promise and had produced a tracking device that she now wore everywhere she went.

Melody fingered the small gold earring in her left ear. It looked so dainty and pretty, but Tex had shown her the software and how it showed her location on a map. Despite knowing how it would look to others, it made her feel better. She remembered weeks ago how she'd told him that it would make her feel better knowing he could find her in case the stalker decided to kidnap her.

"I know, Mel. I wish like hell I could do more."

Melody sighed. "You're doing everything you can, Tex. I'm very thankful for all of it."

"But you still feel smothered."

"Yeah."

"Would it help if I told you it was for your own good?"

"No."

"I didn't think so. You have a job today right?"

Not understanding where Tex was going with the question, Melody answered anyway. "Yeah, in about two hours. Why?"

Tex ran his hand though his hair and looked at Mel. "I thought maybe you could go to the library to do your thing today."

Melody could feel her heart start to beat faster. "Where will you be?"

"I've got some things I need to take care of today. You know I'm retired, but I... help other military teams out and they need me today."

Melody eyed Tex. "You know I'd never tell anyone anything about what you might say or do in my presence."

"I know, that's not what this is about. I don't give a flying fuck if you hear what I do or not. I think you know by now I don't exactly work by-the-book, but I trust you, Mel. I'd rather you stay here, inside, where I know where you are, where you're safe, but I also know you need some space. The library, in public, is the safest place I can think of to give you the space you're craving."

"Thank you. I'd love to go there to do my gig today."

"But you don't take that earring off, you keep your phone close at hand, if anything out of the ordinary happens, I expect you to call me right away."

"I will, Tex. Don't worry. I will."

Tex walked over to the table and sat in the chair next to Melody. He took her hands in his and kissed them. "How are you holding up really?"

"I hate it. How come we can't figure out who's doing this? I mean is he really that smart? You've seen the letters he won't stop sending. Hell, even Amy got one the other day, and that scares me more than anything. I don't understand what he means by, "*You'll pay.*" Pay for what?"

Melody thought about the letter she received just that morning. It'd been taped onto her door. Tex had found it when he walked Baby.

You're a bitch. You'll always be a bitch. You might have others fooled, but I know you. You don't deserve anything you have in your life. You're going to pay for what you did. You better continue to keep that dog on a short leash. If you think that crippled excuse for a man will save you, you're delusional on top of everything else. Prepare to pay.

Melody shivered. "He continues to threaten everyone I love, including you, and I don't know how much more of this I can take, Tex. I just want it to end!"

Tex felt as if his heart stopped beating for a second, then it started again with a thud. He had no idea if Mel realized what she'd just said or not, but he knew her words would be forever engrained on his brain.

"We're closing in on him, Mel. He's getting more careless. We found a fingerprint on the last note. You know they only arrive in the middle of the night, so I'm fairly sure you'll be okay in the library today. But I swear to God, I'm doing everything in my power to make sure he doesn't touch one hair on your head."

Tex waited for her to nod. When she did, he leaned closer to her. "And, Mel, this might not be the time or the place, but I can't keep it in anymore. I love you. I love everything about you. I love how you scrunch your nose in your sleep. I love how you talk to Baby as if she can understand you. I love how you put everyone's well-being before your own. I love how you matter-of-factly help me with my leg every night. You don't make a big deal out of it because to you, it's *not* a big deal. I love how you can type a million words a minute and you don't think it's amazing. I love how you know everyone in this town and you say hello to each and every one of them. I love how you turn the other way when you know I'm doing something that isn't quite legal. Basically, I love everything about you. When this is over, if you still want me, I'm moving up here. I couldn't give a rat's ass where I live, as long as it's with you."

Tex's words seemed to echo in the room. Melody could only look at him in wonder. She didn't think she'd ever hear those words from him, and he'd done so much more than just say the words. "I love you, Tex."

"I know."

Melody smirked. "You're a jerk."

"Come here." Tex tugged Mel out of her chair and pulled her into his lap. She straddled him and ground down against his erection. "I know we don't have time for this right now, but tonight, I'm going to show you just how much I love every inch of this body." Tex ran his hands up and under her shirt at her back and stroked the sensitive skin at the small of her back.

"Only if you'll let me do the same."

"Fuck yeah." Tex leaned forward and kissed her on the forehead.

Melody smirked. She loved it when he did that. It was a secret communication between the two of them now. Each time he did it, she knew he really wanted to throw her down on the nearest flat surface and have his way with her.

"All right. I'll take Baby with me today. You go to the library. Sit out in the common area where the people are. Don't go in the back to the private rooms. You'll be able to concentrate enough out there?" At her nod, he continued. "Okay, I'll drop you off and come back three hours later. I know three hours isn't enough, Mel. I know you wish you could do what you want, when you want, and where you want. I swear we'll get there, but for now, please, for me, take every precaution you can."

"I will, Tex. I swear."

"Okay, let's get this show on the road."

MELODY CONCENTRATED ON the last announcement being made at the meeting she was listening to over the Internet and typed what she was hearing. The voices from the other patrons in the library had faded the moment she'd put in the headphones and started concentrating on typing.

When Melody had arrived at the library she'd said hello to Meredith, the librarian, a woman she'd known her entire life and had settled down at a table to read the latest romance book by her favorite author. She hadn't had time to get through it yet because when she and Tex were home, most of the time he'd interrupted her... not that Melody was complaining. She read for a while then fired up her computer to get to work.

Melody looked up and saw Diane, from the bank, sitting next to her. Melody held up her finger, in the universal symbol for "hang on," as she finished up the presentation. She signed off the closed caption app and popped the headphones out of her ears.

"Hey, Diane."

"Hey, Melody. How are you?"

"I'm good." Melody wasn't quite comfortable talking to Diane, other than the usual pleasantries, because she didn't really know her. There was also that whole dating an ex of hers thing as well. Melody thought back to the information Tex had learned about Lee and felt some of her unease about the woman fade. She felt bad Diane had to live with him. No one deserved to be abused.

"That seems really interesting. I've never seen anyone type so fast before in all my life."

"Yeah, well, I'm actually typing in shorthand, it gets

translated and fed back to the people who have the app."

Diane seemed really impressed. "Well, it's really cool. I'm sure the deaf people really are thankful."

"It feels good to be able to help people." Melody said, looking down at her watch and ignoring the less-than-politically-correct statement from Diane. "Well, look, I gotta get going. My boyfriend will be here in a bit to pick me up."

"Yeah, I've seen him around. He's hot." Diane didn't seem to notice Melody's unease at the turn in conversation.

"Look, I don't mean to be rude, but aren't you seeing Lee? I'm not that comfortable with you talking about Tex that way."

"Oh, I'm sorry. I didn't mean anything by it. Anyway, I just wanted to let you know that I admire you. Seriously. You're doing great things for people and you seem to have a great life."

"Thanks, Diane." Melody looked up and thankfully saw Tex sitting in his truck outside. They'd recently gotten his truck back from the shop. They'd cleaned the paint off and replaced all the tires. She'd missed being able to sit right next to Tex as he drove the rental car and being able to have Baby between them when she was allowed to accompany them.

Melody stood up and gathered her laptop and book.

"He's here. I'll see you around."

"Maybe we can get together for lunch or something sometime?"

Diane seemed eager to be friends, that was obvious. Melody knew what kind of jerk Lee could be. She'd been lonely before too. "Sure. I'll call and we'll set it up."

Diane smiled widely. "Cool! See you around!"

Melody waved at Diane as she walked to the front door. Diane waved back and turned to head into the romance section of the library.

Melody smiled as she walked up to the truck. Baby was sitting in her usual seat in the front. Tex hopped out as she got to the truck to open her door, as he usually did. Melody had tried to tell him not to bother getting out, that she could open her own door and get into the vehicle on her own, but he'd just smiled and ignored her. Just as Melody reached Tex, they heard her name being called from a few spaces away.

Both Tex and Melody turned to see Robert Pletcher stalking their way.

"What the fuck, Melody?"

Melody took a step backward and bumped into the side of the truck. She heard Baby growling from inside.

"Watch it, Robert," Tex warned, putting one arm out and pushing Mel behind him a bit.

"Who the hell are you and how do you know my

name?"

"We've met. When Mel first came back to town."

"Oh yeah, I remember now. You're the possessive fucker who couldn't keep your hands off her in the middle of town. I have no idea what she sees in you, some crippled asshole who's pretending he's infatuated with her. She's not that good of a lay, I'm sure you've figured that out on your own by now."

The words had barely left his mouth when Tex had him on the ground, his knee at his throat and Robert's arms locked against his sides by Tex's hands. "Calm the fuck down, man."

Robert struggled in Tex's hold, but it was obvious he wasn't going anywhere until Tex let him go.

"Care to explain what your problem is, buddy?"

"My problem?" Robert looked up at Melody who hadn't moved away from where she had plastered herself against the side of the truck. "Melody, what the fuck did I do to you? You think it's funny to ruin my marriage?" His voice came out as a croak because of the knee in his throat, but it obviously wasn't completely cutting off his air since he could speak.

"I don't know what you're talking about, Robert. I haven't seen you in ages besides when I got back into town."

"Don't give me that shit. I saw the note you gave Sheri. You told her all about Brooke. Brooke didn't mean shit. She was just a way to get off. Sheri's had three kids and hasn't lost the weight. The sex isn't all that great anymore. I needed more. That's *all* it was with Brooke. But now Sheri wants a divorce and it's all your fault!"

"Enough talking, asshole." Tex put more pressure on Robert's throat to shut him up. "First of all, Melody didn't write you any damn note. She has way too much class for that. She's moved on and doesn't give a shit about you and where you're sticking your dick. Secondly, cheating on your wife is an asshole thing to do. If the sex wasn't good it was your damn fault for not taking care of your woman and making her feel sexy and desired. So who else knew about your affair? It's obvious someone else knew and informed your wife."

"Melody signed the damn note, asswipe," Robert squeaked out.

Tex heard Melody gasp behind him. Dammit.

"And I'm telling you she didn't write it. Are you a handwriting expert? You've never thought that anyone could've signed Melody's name to it? It's all a moot issue anyway. You're missing the point. The point is that if you're sneaking around behind your wife, it's only a matter of time before she finds out. Looks to me you're getting what's coming to you."

Melody watched as Tex leaned down and whispered something in Robert's ear. She couldn't hear what he said, but Robert went still under Tex's body. Tex stood up with more grace than people with two uninjured legs probably would, and seemingly unconcerned about what Robert might do in retaliation, turned his back to him. Robert lay still on the ground, making no move to come after either Melody or Tex.

"Come on, Mel, let's go home." Tex opened the door of the car and urged Mel to climb in. She did and Baby whined next to her.

Tex got in behind her and started the engine. Robert had finally gotten up off the ground and was stalking away from the truck without a second glance.

"What'd you say to him?"

Tex thought about lying or just flat out not telling her, but she needed to know the person he really was. "I just let him know that as a former Navy SEAL I know twenty ways to kill a person that won't leave a mark. And furthermore, I know people who owe me favors who wouldn't hesitate for a second to get rid of his body where no one would ever find it."

"You did not." Melody's voice was low and shocked.

"I did." Tex glanced over at Mel and quickly looked straight ahead again. "I won't apologize for it, Mel. He was an asshole. And I wanted him to know that he couldn't accuse you of shit like that and get away with it. You might not get this, but I hope to hell you're starting to, but that shit won't fly with me. *No one* insults you and gets away with it. He knows you're off limits now."

"What if he's the stalker?"

"Then he knows that I'll protect you with my life. But I honestly don't think he is. If he was, he wouldn't have pulled something so stupid in public. He'd wait and send another fucking letter or something. But if he *is* your stalker, I hope to God he got the point and he'll stop it. But, Mel, I don't think it's him because it's obvious whoever has been after you, wrote that note to his wife and signed your name." When Melody didn't say anything after his announcement he looked over at her. She looked devastated.

"So now he's trying to get everyone to hate me. Is this ever going to end?"

Tex glanced at Mel again as he pulled out of the parking space and headed for her apartment. "Yes, it's fucking going to end. I'm done with this shit." Tex hated to see Mel trembling. She was clutching her hands together in her lap. Baby whimpered and put her head in Melody's lap, as if she understood the stress her mistress was under. Taking one hand off the steering wheel he put it on the back of Mel's head.

"I just don't understand how someone could hate me so much and want to hurt me, my friends, and everyone I love. Why Tex? What did I do?"

"You didn't do anything Mel. It's *him*. *He's* the one

who's fucked up. I'm going to find him. I'm done dicking around."

Melody didn't lift her head. She was at her breaking point. "Maybe I should just go."

Tex's hand flexed on the steering wheel, and he willed the hand on the back of her head not to clench, but he stayed silent. This wasn't the time or the place for this conversation, but they'd be having it… soon.

Chapter Fifteen

M ELODY WENT THROUGH the motions once they'd arrived home. What had been a good day, she'd felt free for the first time in months, had turned into just another nightmare that was her life. She wasn't close friends with Robert, but they'd parted on good terms and she'd never had any issues with him.

The stalker was making it so she never wanted to leave her apartment. Melody had been completely serious when she'd suggested to Tex that she leave again. She couldn't keep going through this. Melody had no idea what Tex really thought about it because he hadn't responded to her suggestion and he'd been quiet since they'd arrived home.

He took care of Baby and had even made her a quick dinner. He'd kept their conversation light and if she was honest with herself, it was freaking her out. Melody was deathly afraid he was going to decide she was too much trouble. It's what, she was ashamed to admit, she'd think about doing if the situation was reversed.

"Go get ready for bed, Mel. I'll be there in a bit."

Melody didn't argue. She padded down the hall to their room and for the first time in a long time, put on a T-shirt and boxers to sleep in. She hadn't been bothering to wear anything to bed because Tex always stripped whatever she'd been wearing off of her the second he came to her.

A while later, Melody watched as Tex padded into the room, Baby at his heels. He went into the bathroom and Baby jumped up on the bed. Melody smiled as her dog turned in about twenty circles, pawing at the covers until they were exactly how her little doggie mind deemed as perfect.

It was obvious Tex wasn't planning on making love to her since he'd let Baby in. Even after all the sex they'd had all over the apartment, he still wasn't comfortable doing it with Baby lying on the bed with them.

Tex came out of the bathroom with a pair of boxers on and sat on the side of the bed. He leaned over and expertly removed his leg. He pushed the covers back and got under the covers.

"Tex... your leg."

"Forget about my leg tonight. It'll be fine without being massaged for one night. Come here, I want to talk to you, but I want to do it when you're in my arms."

"You can talk from there."

"Screw that." Tex moved and pulled Mel into his arms. She fought him for a moment before finally sighing and melting into him. Tex put one of his hands on the back of her head and the other he curled over her waist and held her to him.

He held her to him for a couple of minutes, hating they weren't skin to skin, but understanding why she felt vulnerable tonight and why she'd put on the T-shirt armor.

"Seven months ago when I messaged you, I had no idea it would change my life. But that's what you've done, Mel. You've changed my life. I was only half living before I met you. You forced me out of my own little world, full of self-pity, sitting at home in front of my computers, and forced me to pay attention to what was going on around me.

"If you want to get out of here, go into hiding, no problem. But I'm coming with you. I've got the skills and connections to keep us hidden forever. We can keep on the move, never staying in one place for long, staying safe. But if we do it, you can't keep in touch with Amy or her kids. It would put all of us in danger. Same with your parents. Eventually you'll outlive them, but you can't come back for their funeral. It'd be too danger-ous." Tex let his words sink in.

"You're being manipulative, Tex."

He smiled against her head. He knew she was smart

and would know what he was doing. "I know, but I'm also being honest." After another pause, Tex continued. "Or you can let me do my thing. I've been waiting for this asshole to make a move, but that's over. I'm done fucking around with this guy. I've got some tricks up my sleeve. I can end this. But I'm serious. If you want to go, we'll go."

"Just like that?"

"Just like that."

"You know I don't really want to leave."

"I know."

"A part of me wants to run. Run so far that I don't have to deal with any of this. I have no idea how someone became so obsessed with me that he wants to make me completely miserable. But I want a life with you, Tex. I want to wake up morning after morning to you kissing me and saying you're going to work out. I want to rescue more dogs and give them all a better life. I want to see Cindy and Becky grow up and become amazing women. I want to get drunk with Amy and not have to worry about some psycho spiking my drink or trying to hurt us because of some perceived slight. And every pore in my body wants you, Tex. I want you to bury yourself so far inside of me that I can't think about anything other than you. That I can't feel anything other than you. That I can't remember anyone's hands on me except for yours."

"I can give you all of that, Mel. Fuck. *Please* let me give that to you."

"I'm yours, Tex. I'll go where you want me to go, I'll do what you want me to do."

Tex rolled until Mel was under him. "I want you to be safe and I'm going to make it so. But one thing's for sure."

"What's that?"

"You and Amy will never be able to get drunk in a bar and not have to worry about someone spiking your drink. Two gorgeous women drunk and sexy as fuck? Yeah, not happening. But I'll promise you this. I'll let you get drunk with your friend... as long as I'm there to keep watch."

"Deal."

Melody smiled up at Tex. "You always make me feel better."

"Good. Take off your shirt."

"But Baby..."

"I think we've already corrupted her, Mel. There's no way I'll let Baby keep me from loving you. She'll just have to get used to it."

"Doggy voyeur after all?"

"Guess so. Shirt off."

Melody shimmied under Tex and managed to get her shirt over her head. Tex had come to bed with only his boxers on, so he was already shirtless.

"I love your body. You're soft in all the right places." He cupped her right breast with his hand. "And you're hard in all the other right places." His thumb ran over her nipple, flicking it until it stood up as if begging for his touch.

"I love you, Mel. If push comes to shove I'd give my life for yours."

"No, don't say that!" Melody exclaimed in horror.

"It's true."

"Please, don't. I know you're used to protecting people and you're prepared to give your life for your country and all that. But I wouldn't be able to live if you got yourself killed saving my life. Don't you get it?" Melody grabbed Tex's head in her hands and willed him to understand. "You might think that sacrificing yourself is the ultimate act of love, but it isn't. I don't want to live if you can't too. How would you feel if I told you I'd die for you?"

Tex leaned down, dislodging her hands from his face and kissed her hard. "I'm not going to die, and you aren't either. We'll both make a pact right here and now that neither of us will do something stupid if push comes to shove. Trust me to know how and when to make a move without getting either one of us killed. Okay?"

"Okay."

"Now, lay back. I'm going to take my time tonight.

I know you started on the pill after you got back home. I'd love nothing more than to come inside you tonight without the damn condom between us, but you know I'll use one every day for the rest of my life if it's the only way I can be inside you."

"I want you, just you, in me. I didn't know how to bring it up."

"Consider it brought up, discussed, and agreed upon."

Melody smiled at Tex. She shivered in anticipation. "I can't wait to feel you in me."

"And I can't wait to feel both of our juices coating my cock. You're going to be hot and wet and after I come inside you, you'll be filled up to the rim."

"Uh, that's kinda gross, Tex."

"No, it's not, it's beautiful. I plan on painting both our bodies with our essence. You'll love it as much as I will. I swear."

"I love anything you do to me, Tex."

"I love you, Mel."

"I love you too."

"Now, put your hands above your head and don't move them. It's time for me to play."

Melody smiled and did as she was told. She felt Baby move, but soon didn't think about anything but Tex. His hands, his mouth, his body. And he was right. After they'd made love, and after he'd come inside her, it *was* beautiful. Their combined juices he massaged into both their bodies was sexy as hell. She'd never forget this night. She never felt closer to anyone before, and it'd be forever burned into her brain.

Chapter Sixteen

MELODY HELD TIGHT to Baby's leash as she walked her around the yard of the apartment complex. The stalker was escalating. That morning when Tex had gone out to his truck, he'd found a stuffed dog tied to his bumper by a noose around its neck. Even the cops were alarmed by the note that had been attached to it.

Roses are red, Violets are blue. Baby will be dead, and so will you.

As far as poetry goes, it was awful, but the meaning behind it was clear. Before the notes had just been vague grumblings about how someone didn't like her, but they'd moved into threats.

Melody sighed, remembering the dead cat that had been sitting on Tex's truck the morning before. The stalker was escalating and quickly. Tex had been right, his being around was obviously more than the stalker could deal with.

There were other things that had happened too. The

electricity in Melody's apartment had been cut off. When she'd called about it, she'd been told she hadn't paid her bill. It had taken an hour on the phone with several different customer service agents, and finally a supervisor, to set it straight. Somehow her automatic payments had stopped going through. Melody had managed to give them her credit card to pay for all the missed payments and they'd been appeased, but both she and Tex knew this was just another thing the stalker had somehow done.

Two days ago Tex had convinced Amy to leave town for a week to go on vacation. She and George had taken the girls and they'd headed to Virginia Beach. Tex had set it all up for them. Amy had called Melody completely freaked out because she'd received a box of roses that morning, but when she opened the box, every bloom had been cut off the stem. Then her husband had said his boss, Sam, had received a phone call accusing him of sexual harassment on the job, and the last straw had been when Becky and Cindy had come home from school, each with a package addressed to them that had been sent to the school. The principal had examined the packages before they'd been given to the children, and hadn't seen anything to be worried about. But Amy had taken one look at the note that had accompanied the box of toys and candy and called Melody and Tex.

The note in the kids' boxes were identical and said

merely:

> *Kids are so innocent, it's so sad when something*
> *tragic happens to them. Here's to hoping you never*
> *have to experience that.*

After calling the police and getting all of the incidents documented, Tex had pulled out his laptop and suddenly Amy and her family had an all-inclusive trip to the beach planned, and paid for, by Tex. It was apparent how shaken up Amy was, because with only a token argument about the cost, she'd agreed to go.

Melody hated this. She was no long merely scared, she was pissed. No one had the right to do this to her. It'd be one thing if she was a terrible person and had been a bitch to people left and right, but she had no idea why someone thought she deserved this and wanted to see her hurt... or dead. It made no sense. Tex had grilled her night after night about why someone might have it in for her and Melody honestly had no idea why.

She'd told Tex every single thing she'd ever done in her life in the hopes that something would pan out and would make sense, but Melody knew that nothing she'd said had uncovered any leads. She now had absolutely no secrets from Tex. It was certainly one way to accelerate a relationship.

Tex knew about the two suckers she'd shoplifted from the local gas station when she was seven. He knew about the three cigarettes she'd smoked at a party in high school and how she'd puked for two hours when she'd gotten home. He knew what Halloween costumes she'd worn for the last ten years, he knew the names of her contacts at her job, and even more intimate details about her relationships with the men she'd dated.

The fact was, she had no idea what she'd been missing until Tex made love with her. Sometimes he let her lay there and allowed him do what he wanted to her, sometimes he made her do all the work, both on him and on herself. He worshiped her body and made her believe she was beautiful. She'd never thought she was ugly, but Tex had made her see she was beautiful no matter what her size was. He'd spent hours convincing her. She had no issues anymore walking around the house naked, sleeping naked, or even showering with Tex any chance she got. Basically, Tex had awakened her sensuous side and every time they made love, somehow Tex made her fall in love with him even more.

So here she was, walking Baby and wondering what was next. What the hell could the stalker do next? Would he pop out of a bush with a gun? Would he get a sniper rifle and come after her from afar? A car crash? Tamper with her brakes? There were a million things Melody could think of, none of them good. Tex had let her go outside and walk Baby by herself with a promise she'd come right back inside and she'd never be out of sight of the window to her apartment. Even now Melody knew Tex was watching her from the kitchen. He'd been on the phone when she'd left, talking to someone named "Ghost" and trying to call in some marker or another to try to end the hell they'd been going through.

Melody was so lost in her thoughts, and the routine of walking her dog, that she didn't realize Baby was straining to get something in the grass. Melody had tried to train Baby to leave things alone when she was walking her, but as a hound, it was almost impossible.

Melody pulled back on Baby's leash just before she could snatch up whatever was in the grass. "Forget it, Baby, I feed you, you don't need to eat random crap you find in the yard." She shortened the leash by wrapping it around her hand and took a step closer to whatever it was, trying to see what the hell had Baby so worked up.

She took one look and stepped back quickly. She stared in horror, not believing what she was seeing and spun around to run back upstairs. Baby ran after her as she jogged, thinking they were playing.

"Tex! Tex!" Melody burst into the apartment and looked around.

Tex met her at the door, obviously having seen her quick retreat from the dog walking area through the window. "What? What's wrong? Are you okay?" He examined her from head to toe to try to see if she was hurt.

"Outside… Baby…"

"Slow down, Mel." Tex took her by the shoulders and hauled her into his arms. He kept his eyes on her face, but ran his hands up and down her back, trying to soothe her. "Tell me what happened."

"I was walking Baby and not paying attention… she… she tried to get something in the grass. I pulled her away in time… I'm pretty sure… but Tex… it looked like a steak. An uneaten freaking steak. That *cannot* be a coincidence! Steaks don't just appear in thin air. Not in the pet walking area."

Tex's jaw ticked as he clenched it. "Okay, I'll call the cops again. You stay up here with Baby. Do we need to take her to the vet? You're sure she didn't get any of it?"

Melody sighed. She was so thankful Tex was here to take care of this for her, and that he was worried about her dog. "Yeah, I pulled her away as soon as I noticed her smelling near there. I think she's fine. But what if there's more?"

"I'm going down. I'll look around. Make sure so no one else's dog eats anything."

They looked at each other, remembering the threat from that morning. The steak was most likely poisoned, and meant for Baby.

"My God." Melody's words were whispered and tortured.

Tex didn't know anything he could say to make this any better. When he'd seen the stuffed dog with the noose around it tied to the bumper of his truck he'd been furious. This had gone on way too long. Mel wasn't sleeping well. She'd had a nightmare last night and all he could do was hold her and let her cry when he'd shaken her awake.

"I'll be right back," Tex told her gently.

Melody just nodded. She felt Tex kiss the top of her head and she moved to the couch when he closed and locked the front door behind him. Baby crawled into Melody's lap and rested her head on her shoulder. They stayed like that until Tex came back into the apartment an hour later.

Tex took one look at the woman he loved sitting so still and sad on the couch and immediately went to join her. Sitting next to her, he enveloped her, and Baby into his arms, and the three of them sat there, soaking up as much love and compassion from each other as they could.

Chapter Seventeen

TWO DAYS LATER, Melody sat at the table typing what was being said at a luncheon for a company in Wyoming. It was an awards ceremony and they'd hired the closed caption company to translate for their three hearing-impaired employees. Melody had long ago learned not to really listen to the meaning of the words she heard, but only for the word itself. It made the work go faster and it was definitely less boring that way.

She refused to let her stalker interfere with her job. It was the only normal thing she had in her life at the moment, and it actually helped her not think about how scared and pissed she was for a few hours each day.

Tex had kissed her on the top of the head and told her he was going to take Baby for a walk and that he'd be back in a bit. After the cops had arrived and said the steak that was found in the yard downstairs had indeed been poisoned, Tex wouldn't let Melody walk Baby by herself anymore. He took the dog to different areas in the neighborhood and made sure he kept her on a short leash, just in case anything else had been left around.

As usual, Tex locked Melody into the apartment and warned her to be safe and not open the door to anyone, even someone she knew. Melody merely nodded, reassuring him she'd do as he said.

Twenty minutes later, she typed quickly, smiling when she heard Tex's key in the lock. She was thankful the ceremony she was translating for was almost over, Tex had promised they'd break in the kitchen counter after he got back from walking Baby. They hadn't yet made love there, they kept getting distracted and even though they'd discussed it and teased each other, it hadn't happened yet.

Melody turned to throw a quick smile at Tex as he entered the apartment. She stumbled over the words she was typing as what she was seeing slowly sunk in. Tex entered the apartment first, followed by Diane. Diane was holding a gun against his side and she had Baby's leash in her hand. She'd twisted it around her hand over and over until Baby's front feet weren't touching the ground and she was coughing against the pressure being put on her throat from the collar around her neck being pulled taut.

Tex's jaw was flexing and he was pissed. Melody had thought she'd seen Tex upset before, but it was nothing like what she was looking at right now. She was looking at Tex the killer, the Navy SEAL. It should've scared her, but instead it calmed her. He'd know what to do. The fact that he hadn't already disarmed Diane said volumes about the threat he thought she posed.

While Melody didn't like what she was seeing, a part of her was relieved it was finally coming to an end. One way or another, this stalking shit was going to end. Here. Today.

Melody's fingers continued typing automatically until Diane barked out, "Stop fucking typing, bitch!"

Melody lifted her hands off the keyboard immediately. She reached up and took the headphones out of her ears. She could hear the speaker continuing to talk, and she knew the people viewing the closed caption would be confused when the words coming across their apps didn't match the ceremony and then just stopped in mid-phrase, but it was obvious Diane was deadly serious.

"Go sit on the couch." Diane gestured to the leather couch with her head, not taking the gun off of Tex. She turned to him now. "Don't get any ideas soldier boy. Go sit at the table."

Melody's mind raced. Diane was separating them, making sure Tex didn't get close to her. Baby whined and Melody looked at her. She was standing on her hind feet trying to take the pressure off of her neck, but Diane wasn't giving her any extra room to breathe.

"Please, my dog. Diane, let her go."

"Shut up, Melody. I'll do whatever the hell I want. I've been telling you for months what was coming, but you're still acting all surprised. How fucking cute. It's too bad you didn't just let your precious *Baby* eat the meat and avoid this, but you didn't, so fucking deal."

Melody inhaled. They'd thought her stalker was a guy. All along they'd been searching for a man. Melody had no idea if Tex had even thought it could've been a woman or not, Amy notwithstanding, but it was a moot point now.

"Why, Diane? Why? I don't even really know you. Why would you do this to me? I thought we were friends."

Ignoring her, Diane waved the gun at Tex again. "Take off your fake leg, asshole."

Tex didn't move and Diane sneered at him. "Yeah, I know all about you, *John*." Tex's real name sounded obscene coming from Diane's lips. She'd obviously done her research. Melody had no idea how she'd found out anything about Tex. That freaked her out more than anything else.

"Take off the fucking leg or I'll kill the dog right now." She wrenched the leash she held in her hand and Melody flinched as Baby yelped in pain.

Tex's eyes didn't leave Diane's, but Melody could see that every muscle in his body was taut. He leaned over and lifted his pant leg until he could reach his prosthetic. "Let go of the dog." Even his voice was low and tight, and incredibly controlled.

He waited until Diane put some slack on the leash and Baby could be heard wheezing again, to pop off the suction on his leg.

Melody had no idea what to do. She was completely out of her league. She remembered what seemed like a long time ago telling Tex that even without his leg he was just as lethal as any other SEAL. She hoped like hell he believed it now. All three of their lives were depending on it…on him.

Once his leg was off, Diane ordered, "Scoot it over here to me." Tex shoved it and it clattered toward Diane and came to rest about three feet in front of her. Moving the gun so it was now pointed at Melody, she walked to Tex's leg and kicked it even further away from him, ensuring he couldn't simply fall forward and grab it. "Now sit your ass back down."

Tex did as she asked. Melody knew as long as Diane had the gun pointed at her and had Baby's leash pulled tight, Tex would bide his time.

Diane walked to the couch and leaned over, keeping the gun trained on Melody the entire time. "Stand up." Melody did and watched as Diane leaned over and shoved Baby's leash under the leg of the couch, effectively trapping the dog on a very short lead. Melody didn't like the awkward way Baby had to hold her head, but at least she was on all four legs and could breathe. Diane stood back up and gestured for Melody to sit back down.

Melody tried again to engage Diane. "Why are you doing this? Please, talk to me."

Diane rolled her eyes. "Oh sure, *now* you want to talk to me. You never did before, did you? You and Amy, best friends, queens of the school. Talking in your little hashtag language. You thought you were so fucking funny. Well, you weren't."

"This is because of high school?" Melody couldn't believe it. She tried to keep her voice calm. "That was years ago!"

"I don't care!" Diane shrieked the words, obviously losing it. "I looked up to you. I wanted to be your friend, and you completely dissed me in front of the entire school! You made a fool out of me!"

Trying to calm her down, Melody said in a low voice. "I'm sorry, Diane. Really, I'm so sorry."

"For what Melody? You have no idea do you? You're just saying that. You don't mean it. If you mean it, you tell me for what."

Thinking back to the conversation she'd had with Tex about how Diane had spent some time in at the mental hospital, Melody regretted not having him look into it more. She was obviously unstable and whatever had set her off had probably been festering for a while, but more importantly, Diane had decided to stalk her after having a mental break of some sort. That was the only logical explanation Melody could think of for why Diane was standing in her apartment ready to kill her for some imagined slight while they were in high school.

Melody frantically tried to search her mind for anything that could've set Diane off. She honestly had no idea. "Diane, look. I know Amy and I were a little crazy back in high school. We should've been nicer to people, I know that, but whatever I did to you, I was young. I didn't know any better."

Diane's voice lost its shrill tone, but the flat even cadence was somehow more frightening. "I saw you and Amy joking in the cafeteria one day. You'd been nice to me. I dropped my books in the hall once and you helped me pick them up. I thought you were different from everyone else. I thought we were friends. I heard you and Amy talking in that fucking way you had. I walked up and tried to join in. I said, 'Hashtag you look pretty today' and you know what you said?" Diane waited and then laughed bitterly. "You have no idea do you? You ruined my life and you have no clue. You said loud enough for everyone to hear, 'Hashtag Amy do you hear anything? Hashtag annoying underclassman alert.' And everyone around you laughed hysterically. From that day on no one would talk to me. For two and a half years everyone remembered what queen Melody had said. You ruined my life.

"So I decided to ruin yours in return. It took a while, but I did it. I followed you for years, Melody. I studied you. I had to wait until you got back from college, but once you did, I did what I could to learn everything about you. I wrote that letter to Robert. Now he hates you, as he should. I fucked with Amy. I saw my chance when you broke up with Lee. I got him. I won. He likes *me*, not you. You should hear him talk about what a lousy fuck you were."

Melody tried not to hyperventilate. Diane *was* crazy. She'd built up everything bad that had happened in high school and her life and blamed her. It made no sense. Knowing nothing she was saying was true, Melody tried to placate Diane. "I never slept with him."

"The hell you didn't!" Diane's voice was loud and shrill again. "He told me all about it. How you couldn't take his cock down your throat like I can! How you didn't like to take it up the ass, but I do that for him. *Me!* I do everything you wouldn't and he loves *me* now. I used to think you were so smart. I have no idea why I was so jealous of you. God. It was so easy to make you run. All I had to do was threaten your precious *dog*." Diane kicked at Baby, and the dog yelped as Diane's foot made contact with her back leg.

"Please, Diane. Not Baby. Please don't. She didn't do anything." Melody could feel the tears on her cheeks, but couldn't do anything about making them stop. Watching Baby do her best to escape the cruelty Diane inflicted on her was heart wrenching. Melody had rescued Baby from the shelter and a life where she was probably abused just like Diane was doing to her. She couldn't bear it if they got out of this alive and Baby reverted back to her skittish demeanor.

"Shut *up*," Diane hissed. "Fuck. Still so damn stupid. It was so fucking easy to track you. You thought you were so smart hiding in Florida, then running to California. You think I wouldn't figure out you'd have Amy helping you? The second she came into the bank with that Power of Attorney I knew. I kept my eye on her. After she'd take money out of your account, she'd put it the mail, in her own fucking mailbox. She's as 'hashtag stupid' as you."

Melody flinched, but Diane continued.

"It was so damn easy to rattle you. I called in sick and flew across the country to leave you that note. I knew exactly where you were. You weren't hiding. You're a joke."

"So what now?" Tex's voice was hard and flat from the corner of the room, effectively bringing Diane's attention back to him.

Diane whipped her head around to stare at him. "What now? Now she's going to see what it's like to feel humiliated. She's going to regret dissing me that day.

And when I'm done here, I'm going to do the same thing to Amy. She's just as guilty as Melody."

"Amy's gone. You can't hurt her."

"Whatever, soldier boy. I found Melody, I can find Amy. But you know what? I think I'll start with you instead."

"No! Diane!" Melody stood up at the couch and Diane immediately swung the gun her way.

"Sit down, Mel," Tex told her in a stern voice. "Diane—"

"Aren't you just the concerned boyfriend?" Diane interrupted Tex in a sing-song voice. "No, Melody, don't sit. Go into your bedroom and find something to tie your boyfriend up with. I'll give you twenty seconds. If you don't find anything, I'm going to shoot him in the other leg."

"What?"

"One. Two."

Melody whirled and ran down the hall to her room. Fuck. Diane was bat shit crazy and Melody had no idea what to do. She looked around frantically, hearing Diane counting from the other room. She whipped open her lingerie drawer and pulled out couple pairs of panty hose.

"Eleven. Twelve."

Melody wrenched open the drawer next to the bed and pulled out the bondage ropes she'd bought recently.

She'd meant to get them out and let Tex play with her, but it was too late now.

"Fifteen. Sixteen."

"I'm coming! Don't shoot him!"

Melody stumbled back into the living room and could feel a bead of sweat roll down her face. "I'm here!"

"Tie his ass up. And if you don't make it tight, I'll gut your dog and you can watch her bleed and die right now."

Melody looked and saw that Diane had obviously gone into the kitchen and grabbed one of her steak knives. She held a knife in one hand and the gun in the other. Melody knew Diane would kill Baby in a heartbeat. She dared a look at her dog. Baby was intently watching Diane and growling softly. At least she wasn't cowed by her, but Melody didn't have any time to think about Baby, she quickly walked over to Tex and kneeled at his side.

"I'm so sorry," she whispered dejectedly, dropping the items she'd collected from her room on the floor.

Tex didn't say a word, but kept his eyes trained on Diane. Melody took the pantyhose and wrapped his wrists together behind the chair. He sat tense and motionless as she maneuvered his limbs. She then took the rope and tied his hands to the slats on the chair. She wound the rope around his waist and down to his leg. She tied his good ankle to the chair leg. She wanted to keep the bindings loose, but didn't want to risk Baby's life.

"Now back the hell away from him and sit back on the couch, bitch."

Melody did as Diane asked with a pit in her stomach. She had no idea how they'd get out of this. Now that Tex was tied up, she had no clue what to do. He was supposed to be the one to save them. He'd promised.

Diane laughed a crazy laugh that made the hair on the back of Melody's neck stand up. She'd completely lost it and Melody was at a loss as to what she could do to get them all out of this in one piece.

Melody wanted to try to keep Diane's attention on her. Tex was way too vulnerable right now. "So what? Are you going to shoot me? How is that going to humiliate me? Are you going to kill me, Diane? Do you think you'll get away with that? If you shoot me you'll have to shoot Tex. And the second you pull the trigger someone will call the cops. I'm sorry. I'm truly sorry for anything I did when I was a teenager. Please."

"Oh I don't have to use the gun... yet. Besides, yeah, someone will call the cops, but I'll be long gone when they get here." Diane walked over to Tex. She was smart enough to keep the gun trained on Melody the entire time.

"I have no idea what she sees in you. You're pathet-

ic. Look at you. One fucking leg. Disgusting. I'm sure it's all scarred up too. You must have a big dick, but I'm sure she doesn't satisfy you. Jesus, she's cold. Robert's told me all about it."

Diane took the steak knife she'd been holding and held it to Tex's face.

"Diane…"

She sliced down Tex's cheek, leaving a thin red line of blood in its wake. "Every time you say a fucking word, he gets cut." The words were said nonchalantly, as if she was commenting on the weather.

Melody swallowed the bile that rose in her throat. She couldn't just sit here and let this crazy woman hurt Tex. But she had no idea what to do.

"Remember when your electricity was turned off? Yeah, that was me. It's so easy to fuck with you, bitch. Seriously. You had your payments being directly taken out of your account. All it took was two clicks of my mouse and… whoops… those auto payments stopped."

"You did that?"

"Ah ah ah," Diane chided and she took the knife and ran it down the length of Tex's arm. Once more, blood welled up from the slice. This time Melody heard Tex draw in a quick breath, but he otherwise didn't move and kept his eyes on Diane the entire time.

Melody leaned over and put her head in her hands. She couldn't watch. There was no way.

"New rule." Melody heard Diane's words, but didn't raise her head. "Every five seconds you aren't watching, I cut him."

Melody's head came up quickly at that.

"Too late bitch, five seconds is up." Diane took the now bloody knife and put it against Tex's throat. She pressed in and laughed as she made a downward cutting motion.

Melody cried silently. She could see that each cut she made was deeper and longer. At least she hadn't cut horizontally across Tex's throat, but cutting him vertically was just as bad. The blood oozed from his neck and was absorbed into the collar of his T-shirt, turning it obscenely red in moments.

"It's too late for sorry-ass apologizes, Melody. I don't want to hear your fucking sorries."

Diane stepped away from Tex, obviously having tired of messing with him. Melody risked a look at him and could see that all of his attention was focused on Diane. It was as if he didn't even feel the cuts of the knife into his skin.

"I don't want to hear your fucking apologies, but I *do* want to hear you beg. *Beg* me to spare your pathetic crippled boyfriend's life. *Beg* me to save your dog's life."

Melody didn't waste any time, if Diane wanted her to beg, she'd beg. It wasn't a matter of pride, it was a matter of getting out of the situation alive. "Please,

Diane. Don't do this. I'll do whatever you want. Please. I'm begging you. Don't hurt him anymore. Let Baby go. She's innocent in all of this."

"I changed my mind."

Melody's head hurt. She knew Diane was just playing with her. She might have been cutting Tex, but she was torturing *her*, and they all knew it.

"You have a choice. You want him to walk out of here? Well, he won't be walking will he? More like hopping!" Diane laughed like a loon. Melody kept her mouth shut, waiting to hear what horrible choice she wanted her to make.

"Choose. You or him."

"What? I don't understand."

Diane took a step toward Melody and raised the gun and aimed it at her head. She took another step. Then another. Then one more until she was right next to Melody and the gun was resting against Melody's forehead, right where Tex liked to kiss her. "You get to pick. I figure no matter your choice, it'll ruin your life. So fucking choose. Do I shoot you? Or him?"

Melody looked up at Diane in horror. Was she serious? Of course she was serious. She had a gun to her head and Melody could see the evil behind her eyes. There was no compassion there...at all. Nothing that showed Melody any of them would be getting out of the apartment alive. Diane was going to kill them all, no matter what game she was playing now.

"Me, she chooses me." They were the first words Tex had said since Melody had tied him up.

Diane raised the gun she'd been holding at Melody's head and pointed it at Tex. Before Melody could say anything, Diane pulled the trigger. The sound was obscenely loud and Baby yelped then went back to her low growling. The smell of gunpowder permeated the air around them.

"No!" Melody leaped off the couch, but quickly fell back down when Diane swiped the bloody steak knife over her arm, leaving a long gash. Melody kept her eyes on the kitchen table and was relieved to see Tex still sitting upright. Diane had missed. Thank God. Hopefully the sound of the gun going off would prompt one of her neighbors to call the police as she'd warned Diane earlier.

"Shut. The. Fuck. Up. Crip. This is not your choice. It's hers."

Melody held her bleeding right arm with her left hand and stared at the hole in the wall behind Tex. The next shot could take away the man she loved. All he was, all the good he'd done in the world, all the people who relied on him to help them...all of it would be wiped away by a mentally-ill woman with a crazy grudge.

"Now, Melody. I believe you have a choice to make. Would you rather I blow *his* brains out... and you can live. Or I can shoot you in the head, and *he* can live. Choose."

"Diane, you wanted me to beg, and I'm begging. Please, don't do this."

"Too fucking late. *Choose!*"

"Don't do it, Mel." Tex's voice sounded weird.

Melody couldn't tell if it was from fury or a deeper emotion. She looked over at him. Jesus. He seemed to be covered in blood. It was running down his face and his neck and there was even blood dropping on the floor from the gash in his arm. Melody didn't want either of them to die, but she didn't see any way out of what was about to happen. Tex was tied to the chair, *she'd* fucking tied him there, and Diane had a gun pointed at her head. Melody knew Diane would most likely kill Tex after she shot her, but maybe, just maybe her sacrifice would give Tex time to do...something, and he'd be able to get away.

"I love you." Melody mouthed the words to Tex and she watched as his face hardened in fury. Not at her, but at the situation. Beneath the fury, Melody thought she saw a hint of despair. If these were going to be her last moments, she wanted to be looking at Tex when she died. Tex. The man who'd driven across the country to find her. The man who promised he'd always be there for her. The man who she knew would die in her stead in a heartbeat. Melody tore her eyes away from him, suddenly deciding she didn't want to be looking at Tex when a bullet tore through her brain. It was better he didn't watch her life leave her body.

"Me. Kill me, but leave Tex alone."

Diane threw her head back and cackled. When she had herself back under control, she looked Melody straight in the eye and said in a completely normal voice, "It will be my pleasure."

Melody squeezed her eyes shut and lowered her head and waited. She hoped it wouldn't hurt. When push came to shove it seemed she wasn't as brave as she'd always hoped she'd be when it came to her mortality.

Several things seemed to happen at once. Melody heard the knife Diane was holding clatter to the ground. Baby made a sound Melody had never heard come out of her before and Diane cried out.

Suddenly she was knocked over sideways. Melody's eyes popped open but she couldn't see anything because she found herself underneath Tex. He'd leaped from the chair he'd been strapped to and tackled her off the couch. He'd obviously somehow been able to get out of the bindings she'd used on him.

Melody heard a shot and Tex was off of her before she could get her bearings. A loud shriek and a thud echoed through the apartment. The wailing of police sirens getting closer broke through the sudden silence in the apartment. The sound eerily monotonous and still sounding way too far away.

"Mel, I need you to get up and go to the door. Let the cops in. Don't look over here. You hear me? Do *not* look over here," Tex ordered in a low commanding voice, no hint of the loving man she'd come to know over the last few weeks.

"How'd you get out of the rope?"

"I'm a SEAL, Mel. It wasn't hard. I've been trained how to hold my body while being restrained to minimize the effect of the bindings. I'm assuming the cops were your doing? I don't think they would've gotten here so quickly if someone called them after hearing that first shot."

Melody sat up on the floor and leaned her back against the front of the couch, not looking toward Tex. She couldn't seem to get any air in her lungs. She was breathing way too fast and her heart felt like it was going to beat out of her chest. "Yeah, I typed in a quick message to the people at the ceremony I was translating for. I didn't know if it would work or not."

"You're fucking amazing, Mel. It obviously worked. Are you okay? You didn't get hit? How badly is your arm bleeding?" Tex's questions came at her quick and stoic.

Melody did a quick mental scan of her body. Her arm hurt, but she didn't have any other holes in her body that she could tell, so she was pretty sure she wasn't shot. "I don't think so. Of course, I have so much adrenaline going through my body right now I can't be positive, but I don't see any blood other than on my arm, so I think I'm good. Oh my God! What about you? I need to get you bandaged up."

"I'm good. Go on now. Do as I told you. Go to the door and don't look over here. Let the cops in."

"Tex, you're not okay, she cut you." Melody suddenly remembered. "Wait. What happened? Where's Baby?" she breathed.

"Mel, don't," Tex warned sternly.

But it was too late. Melody whipped her head around to where Diane had been standing next to the couch, on the other side from where Tex had thrown her when he'd yanked her off the couch and to the floor, and inhaled. Tex was lying on top of an unconscious Diane, holding both her hands in his, keeping her captive in case she came to before the police showed up. Melody had no idea what Tex had done to knock her unconscious, but it was obvious he wasn't going to give her a chance to get up and threaten them again anytime soon.

Melody looked to his side and couldn't believe what she was seeing. Baby was lying next to Tex bleeding from her mouth and her haunch. Her eyes were open, but staring straight ahead sightlessly.

"Oh God. No. Baby." Melody scrambled up and

crab walked on her hands and knees over to kneel at Baby's side. She raised tear drenched eyes to Tex. "What happened?"

"Baby saved our lives. She gnawed through her leash and attacked Diane. Just as she was about to pull the trigger and put a bullet in your brain, Baby leaped over and bit her on the thigh. Diane turned and shot her to try to get her to let go. I'd already worked through the knots you made, Diane didn't notice because she was too fucking busy torturing you, and Baby's distraction gave me enough time to get to you and then to Diane and disarm her. I'm so sorry, Mel."

"Nooooo. Tex, she can't have killed Baby. She was only trying to protect us." Melody wiped the tears away from her face with one hand and put her head down next to Baby's muzzle. "Oh God, Baby, please. Don't die. Don't. God. I never wanted this to happen to you." Melody put her hand high on her dog's leg where the blood was slowly oozing out. She looked up at Tex. "Look at the blood on her mouth. She got Diane good didn't she?" The words came out as hiccupped sobs, but Tex understood her anyway.

"Yeah, Mel. She got her good. She saved you. She loved you so much. I knew that the first time I met her. When Amy told me you had a dog I knew I had to bring her to you. Somehow I knew you needed her and she'd be important in this whole damn mess."

Melody sobbed harder and put both hands over the hole in Baby's haunch. The dog didn't even flinch as Melody pushed down to try to stop the bleeding. She had no idea if it was futile or not, but she had to do something. She couldn't sit there and watch the life bleed out of her precious dog.

Melody couldn't see what she was doing through the tears coursing down her face, but she babbled on as she watched the red well-up between her fingers as she tried to staunch the scary amount of blood oozing from the coonhound. "Baby never liked Diane. I never thought anything about it. I just thought she was still scared like she was in the shelter when I got her. But there was one time I clearly remember when we saw Diane on the street. She came up to me and Baby growled. I just backed up and laughed it off. I tried to tell Diane it was just because Baby was a shelter dog and scared, and she'd laughed it off. I should've listened. I should've remembered and told you about it, Tex. I'm so sorry, Baby. I should've listened to you."

Tex couldn't stand it anymore. He leaned up and took off his belt. He lashed Diane's hands together tightly and made sure the gun was kicked across the room. Knowing Mel needed him and Diane was out for the count at the moment, he awkwardly shuffled over to her, grimacing at the phantom pains shooting through his leg at the movement. He ignored them and came up beside Baby and Mel.

He put his hands on Mel's shoulders and tried to tug her into his arms.

Mel jerked away from his touch, not losing her grip on Baby. "No! Tex, no. Baby's not dead. She can't be dead. Call a vet or something. Please. We have to try. I can't let her go."

"Mel."

"God, Tex please. I can't lose her. Not like this. I love her, I need her."

Tex couldn't stand the anguish in Mel's voice. He pulled out his cell phone and swiped the screen, leaving a bloody smear across it, which he ignored. He punched in a number and quickly spoke into it.

"Yeah, I need your help. We're good. It's over, but I need a veterinarian, the best you can get a hold of. Baby was shot. Yeah, by the fucking stalker. Bad. Okay. 'Preciate it." Tex stuffed the phone back into his pocket and told Melody, "Wolf's taking care of it."

He watched as she nodded jerkily, but Tex wasn't sure she really heard him.

"Keep the pressure on her leg, but talk to her, Mel. Like you do. She'll hear you. Tell her to hang on."

Tex's heart broke as he watched the woman he loved speak to Baby through her sobs.

"Baby? You're the bravest dog I've ever met. I have no idea what you went through before I found you, but you have to hang on. You did it. You protected me and Tex. You saved our lives. I know you were probably just paying me back for saving yours, but I still need you. There are other bad people in this world and we need you.

"I swear you can sleep on our bed every night. We won't shut you out again. It's obvious you don't care if we make love with you there, so if you don't care, we won't either. I love it when you scrunch the blankets over and over until they're just right in whatever mysterious way you decide. I promise you can come with us wherever we go. Just please, don't leave me. I love you so much, Baby. I never knew how much. Please don't die. Not like this. I need you."

Melody looked down at the blood that was still slowly seeping through her fingers and onto the floor. Baby's eyes hadn't closed, but she wasn't blinking either. It was the most horrific thing she'd ever witnessed in her life. The tears fell harder. She turned to look at Tex. She could see he was as affected as she was at the sight of Baby motionless on the floor.

"What am I gonna do without her?"

A loud knock came on the door. "Police. Open the door."

Tex got up without a word and hopped to the door. Melody watched, absently noticing how even though he was hopping on one leg, he was steady and confident.

All the practice he'd obviously done without his prosthetic had paid off. He was as confident hopping around the room as he was walking.

Tex held his hands up as the police stormed in with their guns drawn. Melody turned back to her beloved dog, not caring what the cops did. She wasn't going to move her hands from the hole in Baby's haunch until the vet got there. Melody couldn't tell if Baby was breathing or not, her hands were shaking too much and the tears prevented her from being able to see clearly. Ignoring the commotion behind her she leaned down to Baby again. She'd continue to talk to her until the vet arrived. Tex said Wolf would take care of it. She trusted him. "Hold on, Baby. Help's coming. Don't die. I love you."

Chapter Eighteen

MELODY SAT IN the circle of Tex's arms and looked around in wonderment. Her little apartment was overflowing with people. She wasn't sure exactly how it had happened, but all of Tex's friends were there as well as four of their women. Caroline couldn't come because she was in the middle of a huge research project and Alabama had a final exam at school that she couldn't miss. Both had sent their profuse apologizes for not being able to be there.

Melody wiped the tears from her eyes. It felt like she'd been crying forever, but she couldn't seem to make herself stop. She'd had one hit after another and now she found herself crying at the slightest provocation.

"I still don't understand what you're all doing here," she said, voice breaking once more.

"We're here because you needed us, Melody," Wolf told her. He was leaning against the wall as if he was overseeing the group. "All it took was a phone call and Commander Hurt helped get us on the next military flight out here. Tex might live on the other side of the country, but he's always been there for us, it's the least we can do for him to be here when you guys needed us.

"Thank you for getting Dr. Gaiser to come for Baby. We appreciate all he tried to do for her."

"You don't have to thank me, Melody. I'm just so sorry he couldn't save that leg."

"It's okay, Wolf. Baby's alive. That's all that matters. And you know what? I've seen lots of dogs get along just fine on three legs."

Tex ran his fingers through Melody's hair. "Besides, we're a matching set now. Me and Baby."

Everyone in the room laughed. Melody closed her eyes. She was exhausted. After being seen in the emergency room for the cut on her arm, and after Tex had been patched up as well—he'd required some stitches, but refused to be admitted to the hospital—she'd spent the last day at the emergency vet with Baby.

Dr. Gaiser had managed to save Baby's life, but the bullet had cut through her femoral artery, and he hadn't been able to save her leg. The first time Baby had woken up and licked Melody's fingers had been completely overwhelming. The doctor had finally kicked her out, telling her to go home and get some sleep. Baby would be coming home sooner rather than later and Melody and Tex would have their hands full keeping her from chewing on her stitches and helping her get used to her new reality.

"So this woman, Diane, was holding a grudge from when you guys were in high school together?" Summer's voice was incredulous.

"Apparently. I had no idea. But it wasn't just that. She had some sort of mental disorder. The specialists who'd treated her in the past recommended she stay on medication for the rest of her life, but after a couple of years she thought she was better and stopped taking them. That's when it really started. She saw me, and how happy I was with my life and suddenly I was the cause of all the bad things she'd had happened to her in her life. And well... you know the rest."

Amy, who'd rushed back to Pennsylvania from Virginia after hearing what had happened, and had also come over to the apartment, chimed in as well. "Seriously, the bitch used me to find out where Mels was. I can't believe it was her. I hardly even remember her from high school, but apparently she remembered us."

Melody blinked and tried to keep her eyes open. She knew it was rude, but she was exhausted. She'd been stressed for what seemed like forever and having the stalker off her back and knowing Baby would be okay, was making her feel lethargic and she knew she was crashing. Worse were Diane's words that kept echoing through her brain. "*Choose, you or him.*" It was a horrible decision to have to make. Melody knew Tex wasn't happy about her choice, and that he'd want to talk to her about it, but she was just so tired.

She vaguely heard voices around her and put her arms around Tex as he picked her up and carried her somewhere. She didn't care where, as long she didn't have to open her eyes or talk to anyone. She felt herself being laid down and she gripped Tex's neck tighter. "Don't go."

"I'll be right back, Mel."

"Mmmm."

Tex walked out of the bedroom and into the living room. "Thanks for coming, everyone. I appreciate it more than you'll know." Everyone nodded, but looked worried. They'd seen how tired Melody was, and how emotionally fragile she seemed.

"How's she really doing?" Dude asked.

Tex took a deep breath. "She's fine. She's tough. I was worried there for a while when we didn't know if Baby was going to make it, but she rallied."

"Is Diane going to make an insanity plea?" It was Mozart that asked.

"Probably, but I have no idea, and I don't care. Mel will testify if she has to, but we'll just wait and see what happens. I know she just wants to move on with her life, with *our* life."

"Tex, we want you guys to move to California. We want you near us."

Tex shook his head at Cheyenne. "I love that you want us there, but, no. We'll be staying here. This is her hometown. Her friends are here, her family is here. She loves this place. I'll be moving up here to Pennsylvania as soon as Mel's ready."

"She's ready now, Tex," Amy said with certainty.

Tex smiled at Amy. "You bringing Becky and Cindy over tomorrow?"

"Yeah, just let me know when she's up and ready. She's had a tough few days. I don't want to rush her."

"Speaking of a tough few days, we're going to get out of your hair," Abe told Tex and came over to shake his hand. "If you need anything, just let us know. We'll probably be heading out in the morning. You don't need all of us here."

"Thanks, Abe. It means a lot to me that you guys came all the way out here."

"SEALs don't leave SEALs behind," Wolf said with a smile, remembering when he'd gotten together with Caroline how much those words had meant to him and his team.

Tex smiled at the SEAL motto. He might not be active duty anymore, but the words rang just as true today as they always had. He put his hand on Wolf's shoulder. "Thanks."

The men slowly left the apartment with their women and Tex watched them go. He felt lucky to have such good friends.

The last to leave was Amy. Tex knew she'd planned it that way and he waited for her to say what she had to say.

"Mels is my best friend. Neither of us had a sister and we became close when we were in grade school. We've been through a lot, and we've always been there for each other. When I got married I knew we were entering a new phase in our lives. I figured we'd grow apart, but Mels wouldn't let that happen. She browbeat me into going out when I was tired, and she forced me to come over and spend some one-on-one time with her. I love her as if she truly is my sister."

She took a breath and cleared her throat then continued, "When she came to me and told me someone was stalking her, it tore my heart in two. I didn't know what to do for her. The reality was that I couldn't do anything. When she called me and said she wasn't coming back because of the stalker, I cried for two days straight. She was hurting and scared and I couldn't help her. Thank you, Tex. Thank you for seeing something interesting in her stupid chat room handle. Thank you for making the effort to go and find her when she deleted her account. I know her. She would've just kept running if she thought I was in danger and me and my family would've never seen her again. You've given me back my sister and I can't ever repay you."

"I didn't do it for payment, Amy."

"I know, but you're gonna get it in one form or another anyway. My kids see Melody as their Aunt. That means you're now their Uncle. You've suddenly become a part of my crazy family. I hope you can handle it."

"I can handle it." Tex smiled, liking the thought of being an Uncle.

"Good. Now, what are your intentions toward my friend?"

Tex chuckled. "I love her. If it was up to me, we'd fly to Vegas tomorrow and get married, but I have a feeling the two of you have probably planned her wedding down to the minute detail."

Amy just smiled at him.

"Can I make a request?" Tex asked Amy seriously.

"You can, don't know if I can accommodate it, we've planned her wedding down to the color of the napkins on the tables after all," Amy quipped.

"I want Baby standing up with us."

"Done."

They smiled at each other and finally Amy told him, "Okay, enough mushy crap. I'm glad that you're okay. I don't know what went down with Diane yet, but eventually Mels will tell me, but I can tell it gutted her in a way that her physical injuries didn't. Give me a hug, and then get back in there with my best friend. Be forewarned, I expect a girl's night out soon, so be prepared."

"No problem." Tex grabbed Amy's wrist and hauled her to him in a bear hug. "Thanks for being such a good friend, Amy." He felt her nod against him then she pulled away.

Tex watched until she got in her car and pulled out of the parking lot, then he closed the door and headed for Mel, without caring about the mess in the rest of the apartment. There would be time to deal with that later, now he needed to hold Mel in his arms and rejoice they were all still alive.

Chapter Nineteen

MELODY SNUGGLED INTO Tex's arms and sighed. She loved waking up with Tex. She vaguely remembered the night before, and was embarrassed she'd slept through all his friends leaving. She opened her eyes to see Tex staring at her.

"You're still here."

"I didn't want to leave you this morning."

Melody smiled. She'd gotten used to him getting up before her, kissing her awake, then heading out to take care of Baby and to workout. Melody was true to her word and had always fallen right back asleep after he'd left.

"I didn't dream it, did I? Baby's going to be okay?"

"Yeah, Mel. She's going to be just fine. We'll go and see her today and see when Dr. Gaiser thinks she can come home."

"Good. I can't wait to bring her home. I miss her."

"Me too. Mel, we need to talk about what happened." When Melody turned her head away from him, he put his finger under her chin and gently turned her head back to him. "I love you, but you made the wrong choice."

Melody knew immediately what he was talking about. "No, I—"

"You did. I told you once and I'll tell you again, I'd die for you. You mean everything to me. I've known my entire life that I could die on a mission. I was ready for that. We went through training in the Navy on how to withstand torture. You, Mel, *you* are the most important mission of my life. I swear to fucking God I can't live without you. If she'd shot you and you'd died, I wouldn't have been able to go on without you."

"Tex—"

"No. You are the most important thing. You always come first. I don't care what the situation is. First in line, first to eat, first to come, first in everything." Tex's voice hitched and he cleared his throat, forcing back the tears that threatened. He was a big tough Navy SEAL. SEALs didn't cry. "When you said you loved me and you turned and told that bitch that you chose yourself, my heart literally stopped. I can't live without you, Mel. I can't."

"Don't you get it, Tex?" Melody said earnestly, hoping like hell he was hearing her. "Everything you just said I felt in my own heart as I tried to decide what I was supposed to do. I can't live without *you*. I couldn't have lived with myself if I'd told her to kill you. I couldn't. It was an impossible situation, a fucked up impossible situation. Please don't hold it against me. Please?"

Tex hauled Mel into his arms as she sniffed. He rested his cheek on her hair and gritted his teeth, feeling more emotional than he could ever remember being in his life. Jesus, they'd come so close to losing each other. Baby truly was their hero. Tex had been about ready to strike out at Diane, but he might not have made it before she got off a shot. Diane had been standing so close to Melody that it was likely she would've killed her before he could've reached Diane to disarm her.

Tex could feel Melody pulling back and trying to control herself. He pulled back and wiped the tears off her face as she reached up and put her hand on the back of his neck. Tex put thoughts of Diane and how close they'd all come to dying out of this mind. Mel was alive and in his arms. That was all that mattered.

"It was nice of your friends to come all the way out here."

"They're your friends too, Mel."

"I guess. I'm still getting used to it. It's just been me and Amy for so long, and when I was on the run, it was only me."

Tex rolled until she was underneath him. "I'll tell you this now, Mel. You're now a part of a big crazy family that includes six SEAL members and their women. Wait… sorry, that's seven team members… I heard Commander Hurt recently got serious with the woman the team went down to Mexico to rescue." At her look of confusion, Tex brushed it off. "I'm sure you'll get the whole long story from the girls later. Anyway, you'll also probably be adopted by the other SEAL and Delta Force teams I help out as well. They'll all drive you crazy before long, I have no doubt." He watched as she smiled. Tex took a deep breath and said what had been in the back of his mind for longer than Melody would ever realize. "I have something to ask you."

"Okay."

"Will you marry me?"

"What?"

"Will you marry me?"

"Oh my God, that's what I thought you said. I thought you were going to ask me something like what I wanted for breakfast."

Tex just smiled and stared down at the woman he loved.

"Yes, John Keegan, I'll marry you."

"Thank fuck."

Melody giggled. "I'm not sure that's the appropriate response."

"Do you care?"

"No."

"I'll get to work today in getting my stuff moved up here. I hope you aren't too attached to this apartment. We really need a bigger place, one with a yard so we can let Baby out and not have to walk her on a leash."

"Uh, Tex—"

"And you'll need to make sure you contact your boss to make sure she's okay with what happened the other day."

"Tex, wait. You're moving up here?"

"Yeah, Mel. You agreed to marry me, Of course I'm moving up here."

"There's no of course about it, Tex. We both have portable jobs, we could go wherever we wanted."

"We could live anywhere, but *this* is your home. I would never take you from Amy, and your parents, and from here. You ran long enough. I'm more than happy to come up here and live with you."

"I love you, Tex."

"I love you too."

"No, I *love* you."

Tex chuckled. "If I remember, we never did get to break-in that counter. It'd be a shame to move out of here before we lived out that little fantasy of ours."

"I think I'm hungry. Care to meet me in the kitchen?"

Tex leaned down and kissed Mel deeply. "We were

made for each other, Mel. You make me feel more of a man than I ever have before. Thank you. Thank you for loving me, for letting me love you back."

"You're welcome. Now, come on, I'm hungry."

The look in her eye was so carnal, Tex could feel the blood pump into his erection.

He couldn't resist. He leaned down and kissed her, holding nothing back. Melody gave as good as she got. She plunged her tongue into his mouth and countered his thrusts with her own. Tex's hand made its way up her belly, under her shirt, until he reached her nipple. As he squeezed the taut nipple she broke her mouth away from his and gasped, throwing her head back.

"Tex."

"That's it, Mel. That's it." Tex could feel her legs trembling against him. He paused long enough to pull her shirt up and off her head until she was bare from the waist up. He'd never get tired of her. "You're beautiful. And mine." He lowered his head until he had one nipple in his mouth. He used his hand to plump up the other breast and to tease that peak until it pebbled.

Tex loved feeling Melody writhe and arch up to him. He took hold of the bud he had between his teeth, and watching her eyes, pulled upward. When she gasped, he let go and watched as she brought her hand up to his face.

"I need you, Tex. Now. Take me."

"We have a date with a kitchen counter. Go on. When I walk in there I want to see you on the counter, naked, legs apart waiting for me. You'll eat soon enough, but I think it's my turn to go first."

Melody smiled as she climbed out of bed and headed for the door. She made her way down the hall to the kitchen. After removing her boxers, she thought about her life. She had everything she'd ever wanted. Friends, family, and now a man who would not only stand next to her, but in front of her when she needed it and behind her when it suited him. He was perfect. She couldn't wait to become Melody Keegan.

Melody sent up a silent prayer of thanks to Diane. In a sick way, it if wasn't for her delusions, Melody never would've met Tex. Everything happened for a reason, sometimes you just had to wait around for a while to figure out what those reasons were.

As Melody hopped up on the counter and leaned back on her hands, waiting for her fiancé, she grinned. Life was good.

Epilogue

"COME ON, BABY, come 'ere girl!" Melody called to her dog and watched with a smile as the dog ran toward her. She only had three legs, but she'd never let it slow her down. From the first day Dr. Gaiser had put her upright in the animal hospital, she'd hopped along like she'd been doing it her entire life. Melody had, of course, cried with joy.

The only difference Melody could see with her dog was that she now never let her mistress out of her sight. Baby would follow Melody around their house, not caring what she was doing, if Melody got up, Baby went after her.

"You ready to go, Mel?"

Melody nodded up at Tex. They'd come to the park to let Baby get some exercise, the vet had said it was important that she not just sit around, but that she exercise her leg and make sure she used her muscles more since they were compensating for the loss of her back leg.

"Let's go home. The girls will be calling in thirty minutes."

The Skype phone calls had started the week after their incident. All the girls would get together out in California and call to talk. Soon it had turned into a free-for-all because the men wanted to be there too. One night the call lasted for three hours. Everyone had laughed and told stories all night long.

Afterwards, when Melody was in bed with Tex, trying to recover after a long love-making session which involved the bondage ropes Melody finally convinced Tex to use on her, she'd commented on the close friendship everyone had.

"Being in the military makes men have a special bond. Combat makes that bond stronger. Being a Navy SEAL means that connection is unbreakable. Those men have been through hell and back, and so have their women. Because of their experiences, they know they have a group of people that will always have their back, no matter what. And Mel, you're a part of that too. I know we don't live out there with them, but they feel it just the same."

"I know, Tex. I feel it. I didn't understand when we were talking online all those months ago. I told you that your friends were taking advantage of you because they didn't come out and visit you. But I get it now. They weren't. Your bond is just as strong from thousands of miles away then if you were right there with them. You're a part of that team. You know it. They know it. The women know it."

"Yup."

"I love you."

"I love you too."

"I have a question for you, and you can say no."

"What is it, Mel?"

"Do you think all your friends will be able to fly to Vegas this month?"

"Why?"

"I want us to get married now."

Tex went up on an elbow over Melody in the bed and put his hand on her cheek. "Why?"

"I want to be connected to you so badly. I just... I need that. I don't want to wait."

"But your dream wedding. You and Amy have been planning this for your entire life."

"Here's the thing, Tex. When Diane had that gun aimed at me and was about to shoot, all I could think about was how much I was sorry I wasn't yours... officially. I honestly don't give a damn about a white dress and all that shit. All I want is to belong to you. And for you to belong to me. I already talked to Amy. We can still have the reception. We'll do that here for all my friends and family, but I want to have the ceremony itself with *your* family. I want to bring Baby and find a chapel in Las Vegas that won't mind if she's there. I want everyone to come and stand up with us. Amy and George will be there with their girls too. My parents said they'd fly out there for the actual ceremony as well. It feels right."

Tex dipped his head and kissed Melody's forehead. "God, I love you so fucking much. When I think about how close we came to never meeting…"

"I know."

"I'll call Wolf in the morning and see when they can get free. We'll drive out there with Baby, but take the time to sightsee along the way without rushing. We'll have the best damn Vegas wedding ever. But know this, you belong to me and I belong to you no matter when or if we get married."

"Damn straight."

Tex smiled. She was so damn cute. "I'm feeling awfully awake now, Mel."

She grinned up at him. "Oh?"

"Yeah. Turn over."

"Bossy."

"Yup, you said it yourself. You can take the man out of the SEALs, but you can't take the SEAL out of the man. Turn. Over."

Melody did as Tex asked, knowing that whatever he had planned meant hours of enjoyment for her. He always took care of her. He was completely serious when he'd told her that she came first in all things.

ON THE OTHER side of the country six Navy SEALs and their women were settling down into their beds for the night. Each couple had been through hell and come out on the other side. Each man had claimed their woman as theirs, and each woman had claimed her man right back. Some people would look at them and wonder how in the hell their marriages and relationships could survive the stress and uncertainty that came with being an elite fighting machine. But if they were asked each one would say it was because of love. They'd seen what life could be without the other and had made promises, spoken and unspoken, that they'd always be together.

And if the women got together when the men left on missions and cried and got drunk, no one told their SEALs, and the SEALs pretended it didn't happen. But ultimately it was the friendship they all had with one another that helped make the separations feel shorter and their love stronger.

In Tex's office, two computers stayed on all day and all night. Seven red dots blinked on a map, six dots in California and one in Pennsylvania. Seven Navy SEALs and women slept easier at night because of those blinking red dots. Some wouldn't understand, but those people hadn't been in their shoes.

Look for the last book in the
SEAL of Protection Series,
Protecting the Future.

See what all your favorite couples are up to
two years in the future.

Discover other titles by Susan Stoker

<u>SEAL of Protection Series</u>
Protecting Caroline
Protecting Alabama
Protecting Fiona
Marrying Caroline (novella)
Protecting Summer
Protecting Cheyenne
Protecting Jessyka
Protecting Julie (novella)
Protecting Melody
Protecting the Future

<u>Delta Force Heroes Series</u>
Rescuing Rayne
Assisting Aimee (loosely related to DF)
Rescuing Emily
Rescuing Harley
Rescuing Kassie (TBA)
Rescuing Casey (TBA)
Rescuing Wendy (TBA)
Rescuing Mary (TBA)

Connect with Susan Online

Susan's Facebook Profile and Page:
www.facebook.com/authorsstoker
www.facebook.com/authorsusanstoker

Follow Susan on Twitter:
www.twitter.com/Susan_Stoker

Find Susan's Books on Goodreads:
www.goodreads.com/SusanStoker

Email: Susan@StokerAces.com

Website: www.StokerAces.com

To sign up for Susan's Newsletter go to:
http://bit.ly/SusanStokerNewsletter

Or text: STOKER to 24587 for text alerts on your mobile device

About the Author

New York Times, USA Today, and *Wall Street Journal* Bestselling Author Susan Stoker has a heart as big as the state of Texas, where she lives, but this all-American girl has also spent the last fourteen years living in Missouri, California, Colorado, and Indiana. She's married to a retired Army man who now gets to follow *her* around the country.

She debuted her first series in 2014 and quickly followed that up with the SEAL of Protection Series, which solidified her love of writing and creating stories readers can get lost in.

If you enjoyed this book, or any book, please consider leaving a review. It's appreciated by authors more than you'll know.